PRINCE OF PINES

by

GERALD BRENNAN

ಽಂಜ

DreamStreet Press
Ann Arbor, MI USA
www.DreamStreetPress.com

ISBN: 978-1-7350802-1-5

to

Pat O'Neill

PRINCE OF PINES

1

John Wheelwright had always been a hard-working man, but a change had come. For more than half of his 30 years he had worked a dizzying variety of jobs in northern Michigan and in the Upper Peninsula, where he lived with his family until he was 24. He watched from his apartment window the belching plumes of black smoke billow from the Oslow Chemical Plant complex about four miles away, near the shores of Lake Michigan. He heard sirens all over town, looked down, and saw the streets choked with traffic from the evacuation.

Though John Wheelwright had worked hard all his life, he found himself watching the lives of others not so lucky fall apart. His own life had fallen apart, and he hadn't even known about it until now. What an idiot he had been! He drained the last of the Coke he had been nursing all morning and threw the plastic bottle into the wastebasket.

He is supposed to feel lucky. He still has a job. The depression has the whole world in its grip, except for the ultra-wealthy who fight among themselves for the spoils. There is a bad war in the Middle East (when is there not?), and violence, civil and/or military, flares on six continents. Most city-dwellers in the USA now live in equal fear of the violent criminals and the police. The most terrifying are the National Police and the red-helmeted foreigners under their jurisdiction. Civil rights have been suspended for two years by the implementation of an executive order formulated two presidential administrations ago. In the rural areas of Michigan, anarchy reigns. Robbery and poaching are the preferred modes of survival there among the resistors and the scum, which are hard to tell apart.

There was a loud rap on John's door. "Wheelwright?" hollered a voice from the hallway.

"What?" John yelled back. It was the superintendent. They shared a vivid mutual loathing.

"Move your ass out of here. The cops want everybody out in two hours."

John looked around at the mess in his apartment. "Fuck all this," he whispered to himself.

"You hear me in there?" the super shouted.

"Piss off, Harvey!" John yelled back and heard the superintendent move away and knock on the apartment door next to his.

John turned on the radio. There was an oldie by Iris Dement playing. *Our Town.* It was the perfect soundtrack to the day. *They ought to just play it in a loop*, he thought with a bitter laugh.

John slumped into his big recliner. A change had come over him, slowly at first as he became more aware of how the world worked, how good people lost their jobs and homes, and watched their children go hungry. These are the ones who refused the National Service jobs that the government offered to the armies of the unemployed. Some of these jobs were the pits, like the Civilian Disarmament Force job that his friend Elliot was offered, for instance. For minimum wage, they were obliged to show their patriotism and goodwill by participating in house-to-house searches for firearms. They refused, and this act, naturally, disqualified them (and Elliot's family) from all government benefits.

But even Elliot, a not terribly bright, go-along-to-get-along sort, knew that this was a very dangerous job, in addition to the moral implications. Many in the disarmament service were killed by their intended victims. Trouble was, when you refused the first job offer, there was no more coming, unless you had connections.

John became aware of how those who had any extra would share the little they had, and he saw that the only people who would not share the burdens of the community in these awful times were among those who had a lot. The sirens stopped, and the Disaster Preparedness System blared the latest information and instructions. John went back to the window and scanned the skyline.

First, the Mackinac Bridge, now the chemical plants. John mused on the string of recent regional disasters. No one ever seemed to know who really was responsible for what. With every new catastrophe, a whole gamut of organizations would proudly claim responsibility, but official blame was always assigned to whatever group the government was most eager to villainize, whether they claimed responsibility or not.

John Wheelwright, like everyone else in the town of Sellick, was obliged by the authorities to evacuate the city, such was the danger of contamination should the wind's direction or speed change, which was indeed in the forecast.

I'm going home, he decided, to the farm of his family in the middle of the Upper Peninsula, where he had not been in six years. Were they still there? He turned from the window and took a brief survey of all he owned, which wasn't much.

John was an Olympic marksman who lost the Gold Medal in a hotly contested match with a smart-assed English kid. He had amassed several guns and trophies, and the trophies were staying behind. He never cared about them anyway. His guns were a different matter. His favorites included an AR-15 that he built himself, an accurized and combat-optimized Colt .45 pistol; a Mossberg pump shotgun, and his .22 Olympic Hammerli pistol.

The change that had come over John was accelerated by the suicide of his friend Elliot. He witnesses the circumstances of the times take this strong family man and cut him down. The lay-off, the job refusal, the drinking, the divorce, the arrests and the beatings – the pattern was a familiar one, for it seemed everyone knew of such cases these days.

In all of John's hardworking days he had never suffered humiliation, but the job he worked lately and until today shamed him. It always had, he realized, but he had not seen it until now, blinded by the work ethic his father had ground into him since he was a child. As long as you had a job you could hold your head up. "Horseshit," he said aloud.

He was employed as a janitor in the offices of Aaron Green, who had a lot, and shared nothing. With the huge number of foreclosures in the region, Green by now owned most of the city. He was not just covetous and miserly, John observed, he was ostentatious. While he watched his friends sink into despair and poverty, he watched the Greens drive, wear, and revel in nothing but the best. The little commerce taking place was Green's commerce. The local police were Green's police. And John worked for this man who was the very emblem of what was wrong with his community, and communities all over the country.

John decided that the time of taking pride in being a hard-working man was over. He wanted to see the pine jungles of his youth again and rejoin the life he had fled. But he couldn't leave without settling a few accounts and lend a hand to those who were close to him these past few years, who were there to stop him from slipping through the cracks and sliding into hell.

It was almost noon. He locked his valuables in his antique gunsafe in case the inevitable looting began before he returned from his errand. He pulled on his shoulder holster, snapped the buckle closed on the big Colt, and slid a couple spare magazines into their little pockets, snapping them secure. It was time to get out from under the yoke. He had grown sick of himself, and it was time to start a new life.

2

John was in luck. With a rush of adrenaline, he noticed that Green's home was lit up, and there were three cars in the driveway. John discreetly pulled his battered old Taurus to the curb, shut the car off, pocketed the keys, and studied the scene. There was a lot of commotion about the estate this morning. A small van which John recognized as being a utility vehicle from the main office was being loaded with a few effects by a couple of burly gentlemen whom John did not recognize. Green was married but had no children, and the missus was nowhere in sight. Neither, John observed after about five minutes, was Green himself, but it was clear that even Green would be obliged to join the rabble for a short exodus from town until the crisis had passed.

At length, the mansion door opened, and Green's wife emerged with what must have been a maid, for she was a trim young black woman, burdened down with the chosen personal effects of the boss lady. Green and one of the burly guys emerged behind the pair of women. Green gave his wife a little kiss, and then the big guy opened the trunk of one of the waiting cars, relieved the maid of her burdens, shut the trunk and assisted the ladies into the car. With a wave they were off, and Green went back into the house.

Now or never, John thought to himself, ducking down in his seat as the car sped by him. There was no way of knowing who, besides Green and one of his men, was inside the mansion. John was relieved that there seemed to be no dogs to contend with.

He got out of the car and opened the trunk, found a pair of gloves and put them on. Next, he checked his shoulder holster rig, tugging at it to achieve some level of comfort (he never owned a shoulder holster that didn't make his neck ache). He put on a ski mask and lifted free the five-gallon can of gasoline, which he placed on the ground. He looked about him carefully and shut the trunk, grabbed the gas can, and set out on his mission.

Coming to the edge of Green's brick fence, which ran about 70 yards before the main gate, John set the gas can down and bolted along the wall, stooping a bit to keep his head below the wall line. At the gate, he peeked around and saw that the mansion door was now closed. *Gotta be a surveillance system*, he thought to himself, but he realized that with all the chaos in town, even Green's problems would have to take a back seat. He took a deep breath, turned the corner, and rushed to the double doors of the pillared mansion.

He paused, looking for cameras and other signs of a security setup, when he heard voices from within growing louder. John braced himself and watched the doors.

It was the big man who emerged, carrying a large box filled with books that he could barely see over. John was still, and the big man never looked to his side. As this fellow (who was much bigger up-close than John had estimated) made his way down the few steps to the driveway, John slipped inside the house. His plan was to wait for the big guy to come back in and knock him silly with the pistol. But the sudden appearance of Green put an end to that nice pat plan.

"What's going on?!" Green froze as he came around the vestibule corner. John leaped upon the old man and clamped his mouth closed while old Green twisted and mumbled pathetically in John's grip. Now footsteps grew louder as the big man tramped up the outside steps toward the door. John dragged Green around the vestibule corner, out of sight of the big man who entered, turned, closed the door, turned again, and walked out of the vestibule.

John thrust Green across the carpeted floor where he collapsed in a heap a few yards away. John drew his .45.

"Carmen!" Green, now struggling to rise, called to the big man. "Stop that man!"

John had his gun at the center of Carmen's considerable bulk. More foolish than fearless, the beefy bodyguard nevertheless advanced upon John, who had no intention of shooting him but realized the seriousness of his predicament. Gorilla-like, Carmen, intimidating but ultimately hapless, grabbed for John's neck, and John retorted with the butt of his pistol against Carmen's thick skull, which gave way with a thud. Carmen fell to the floor.

Green was on the cellphone, but his 911 plea for assistance was useless in the face of the civil emergency brewing back in town. John stood a few feet from the banker, pistol drawn. Green put the telephone down and faced John, obviously very agitated, one hand on his skinny chest.

John made him sit on a big leather couch and within three minutes had zip-tied and blindfolded both Green, fully alert, and Carmen, who was still unconscious on the carpet. John next removed his ski mask and set about the unfamiliar task of ransacking a mansion for easily traded valuables. This was a disappointing endeavor, netting but a few of the expensive knick-knacks of the wealthy, and some jewelry left behind by the little woman. John needed cash. He approached the banker, supine, bound and blindfolded on the large couch.

"Green, I want cash."

"I don't have any."

"Academic, Green; I'll be right back," John said flatly. "Don't go away."

John left the house to retrieve the gas cans and returned directly. He put his ski mask back on and removed Green's blindfold.

"This is a five-gallon can of gasoline."

"What are you going to do? Kill us and burn the house?" the banker said calmly. "Who are you? I recognize you!"

"I won't kill you. But I will burn the house down. And as you know, there are no firetrucks to spare at present."

"I don't have any cash, I told you."

"Look, Green," John was gentle. "I don't care about your goddam house. I want $10,000. For that much, you get to keep the house."

"I'm insured."

"Nevertheless," John was patient. "I *will* burn your house down."

"If I had money, I'd give it to you."

"Too bad," John feigned a sad resignation. "Such a nice, big, house."

John uncapped the can and sprayed gasoline around the room, dousing the concert grand piano and the ceiling-high bookcase with a few flourishing sprays.

"Stop it," the banker hollered. "I'll give you your money." He panted anxiously and looked over with disgust at his bound and insensible bodyguard. "I mean, I'll give you *my* money."

"Green, you are a parasite and a scumbucket," John said quietly. "Where's the money?"

"I worked for everything I have!" Green was foaming mad. "I started from *nothing*! And I did it by the book! And you're nothing but a goddam reptile and a thief!"

"Reptile?" John was impressed. He had been called many things, but, reptile? "And the money is *where* now?"

9

"In the book called *Annals of Imperial Rome*. Second shelf from the top. In there, you'll find your $10,000. I trust you'll leave the rest if you have any honor."

The book retrieved, John opened it and found a portion hollowed out. Inside were one hundred $100 bills. "Best leave honor out of this, Green," John replied. He held up the new bundle of bills. "Kiss it goodbye."

"Where have I heard your voice before?" his captive croaked. The big bulk of Carmen began to moan and stir in its binds. This was a relief to John, who had never sapped anyone before, and worried that he had hit the big man too hard.

"I'll find you," Green said. "I'll find you. And I'll make you regret this. You... goddam lowlife!"

"Consider it a small gift to a few worthy members of the community," John replied with a smile, swung his sack over his shoulder, and left the mansion.

Speeding back toward town, John considered the logistical problems that the rest of the day would present. There were a few stops to make in the city, to some people he knew he would never see again. He carefully drove the old Ford south-bound toward the city, and there was plenty of traffic to hide in, courtesy of the evacuation, but going was slow. John knew that soon there would be an all-points bulletin out on the masked bandit that robbed the town's main man, but John had changed clothes (he cleaned up nicely when it was necessary), knew that he had left a clean scene, that all the lawmen were otherwise occupied, and that there was really no way to connect him to the crime. He said the word aloud.

"Crime. Criminal." John felt justified in doing what he did, but was uncomfortable with having done it just the same. "Robber. Thief. Reptile." Such action was so at odds with his upbringing.

Traffic was thickening as he approached the city and became so bad that he couldn't get within three blocks of his apartment, a condition that could have uncomfortable consequences. He pulled down a residential street full of boarded-up buildings, which sheltered the homeless by night and the drug users by day. Fentanyl had made a big comeback, thanks to Green's organization, and Oslow was filthy with it. Cutting into an adjacent alley, he opened the trunk and took out the sack of money and other negotiables. With the near-panic in the town it was easy to be inconspicuous, so John just strolled the three blocks to the apartment building, whistling and greeting other harried pedestrians.

At his apartment door, the coast was clear, and John sprang up the staircase to his small second-floor suite. Outside his apartment door stood his little friend Jalen, a ten year-old black kid who lived a few buildings down with his aunt and her daughter. Jalen was precocious. He was an excellent talker, an incredible chess player (he beat John always), and a constant hooky player, much to the consternation of his aunt, who had no appreciation for the boy and beat hell out of him regularly.

"I was waiting for you," he said to John, with a big grin.

"I see that," John said, fishing for his keys. "How's it goin', pal?"

"Bad."

"What's wrong?" John asked him as he pushed the door open and ushered the little guy inside, putting the bag on top of his refrigerator.

"What's in your bag?" Jalen inquired.

"Just some stuff. What's the matter? How come you're not with your aunt getting ready to leave town? You gotta go you know," John said as he opened the fridge and grabbed a couple of Cokes. "We all gotta go."

"That's what's bad," Jalen answered, suddenly gloomy. John opened the Cokes and gave one to the boy, who sat on a kitchen chair.

"My aunt is a big fuckin' fat *bitch*," Jalen declared fearlessly.

Jon winced. "I know you don't get along with her, pal. What's the matter?"

"She's *gone*," he said, and burst out crying. Fearing the worst, John pulled up a chair and sat close to him. He took the Coke from his little hands and put it on the table. Jalen got up from the chair, crying in heaving sobs, and put his head against John's chest, who hugged the boy and tried to comfort him. John was uncomfortable with kids, and though he felt a lot of affection for Jalen, he felt clumsy in his attempt to comfort the boy, doing the "there, there… come on now…" thing.

When Jalen had calmed enough to talk he confirmed John's fears. John knew that Jalen's aunt (the boy never knew his parents) had many boyfriends and no money. She used to be a chemistry teacher at the community college, but drugs did her in. There were so many chemical vices from which to choose these days, and his aunt had been intent upon sampling them all. Her current man, who found Jalen even more of a pest than his aunt did, left with her that morning, right after the evacuation was announced. She left a note, hastily scribbled and unsigned, which Jalen showed to John.

Me and Arnold and Sissy are gone.
We will be far away so tell your teacher or the preacher that you need a place to be. You will be better off.

"See?" Jalen asked pathetically. Jalen had never once shed a tear in the five years since they first met in the park over a chessboard.

"I see what you mean," John answered. Even a bitch aunt was infinitely preferable to abandonment. "Here," he handed him a tissue, "blow your nose." Jalen did as he was told.

"Jalen, do you have any family or friends anywhere that you would like to visit?" The lad shook his head.

"How about, eh," John was stumped, "...ah, nevermind. Want your Coke back?"

Jalen nodded, took the bottle and had a sip, then put it down and blew his nose again. John sat down on the couch. *This is not in the gameplan*, he thought. He turned his head and considered the sad little boy on the chair. "Listen, we'll figure something out, okay?"

The boy smiled a weak smile. He intuited that if John stayed close, then everything would be all right.

"I need to see a couple of people in the building right now. You wanna watch TV or play video games for a little while?"

"TV sucks," Jalen replied, but he knew John needed a break. "But I'll watch it anyway."

"There's a good little American boy," John joked and poked Jalen in the belly with his finger, coaxing a little laugh. "I'll be back in a few."

As John reached the door, Jalen shouted in a panic, "John! You're really coming back, right?"

John smiled and nodded. Jalen blew his nose.

On the fourth floor of the building lived the Preston family. Mr. Preston had taken him hunting and fishing since he arrived downstate, and Mrs. Preston enjoyed cooking for John, which for a bachelor is often a blessing indeed. Both the Prestons enjoyed John's company, and he loved them dearly. Their three children had fled the nest but were frequent visitors, and John liked them, too. They shared a lot these past few years. John hoped, as he turned the corner to the last stretch of hallway, that they had not yet evacuated.

They hadn't. He could hear them behind the door, on which he tapped with his knuckles. The door swung open to the sweet face of Mrs. Preston, damp washed brown locks all curly.

"John, my dear," she smiled and gave him a hug. "Did you hear the news? Isn't it awful? What are we all going to do?" She ushered him inside.

"For Christ's sake Enid, give the boy a break," Mr. Preston, in tee-shirt and pajama bottoms, stepped out from the bathroom long enough to display his half-lathered face and give John a little wink. "He just got here. Get him some coffee for Christ's sake."

"Do you want coffee, dear?" Enid asked and motioned toward the sofa. "Sit down and I'll bring you some."

"Thanks, Enid, I could use a blast, I guess."

John sat and sipped hot java, and Bill Preston re-emerged from the bathroom, wiping the last bits of shaving cream from his neck and nostrils with a white towel. "Can you believe those sons-of-bitches?" he asked John rhetorically and fell into the big chair near the front window. He opened a drawer and pulled out a couple of cigars. "Want one?"

"No, thanks. I can't enjoy it today, I'm afraid."

"Where are you gonna go? Come with us?" Bill asked, unlit stogie hanging in his lips like he was born that way.

"I'm going up north to see my family, Bill," John said, "but thanks."

"I'm going to give you our address, John, and I don't want you to lose it," Enid said, scribbling on a notepad. "You come see us if things don't work out, now. And if they do, then you come see us anyway," she giggled at her little joke.

John took the paper and stood up. "Listen, Enid thanks for the coffee, but I can't stay. I came to give you a little going away present." John reached into his shirt pocket and brought out ten $100 bills and put them on the coffee table. "This is for you."

"I can't accept it," Bill said flatly. "You crazy bastard, *what did you do?*"

"My God, Johnny, where in the world..."

"Where did that come from?" Bill interrupted his wife.

"Listen," John began, not sure quite what to say. "You lost your house when the bank foreclosed. Well, I ran into some money. Quite a lot of money. And this is for you."

"How did you get it?" Bill was direct, as always.

John took a deep breath. "I took it from Green," he said flatly. "Like he took it from you."

"O Johnny..." Enid was, what? Disappointed?

"Listen: if I had the brains and balls to steal that money from that son of a bitch, I'd have done it for myself." Bill stood up and placed a big hand on John's shoulder. "I don't blame you for doin' it. Shit, I *love* you for doin' it. I just can't take it from you."

John understood. It wasn't a judgment against him.

"It was sweet, dear," Enid assured him. "But aren't you afraid you'll get caught?"

"No." John stared at his shoes. "I did it right."

"I'll bet you did, Johnny," Bill said with a smile.

"Well," John shuffled uncomfortably, "I got a lot to do..."

Bill held out a big paw. "We'll miss you. Come see us, eh?"

John slapped his hand away and gave him a bear hug. *No more huntin' with Bill,* he thought sadly as Bill pressed him hard. John turned to Enid.

"You'll visit, now, won't you?" she asked him as John embraced the slender and delicate Enid, and kissed her smooth cheek.

John promised he would visit, or at least write to them soon to let them know he was alright, but in his heart he knew that he would never see again. As he left the apartment, John dropped the wad of bills on the floor and gave it a discreet kick along the wall. This was futile.

"Hey!" John called. "Get back here, you sneaky bastard." And John picked up the wad of cash and stuffed it into John's shirt pocket. "I was watchin' for tricks. Now git." His fake anger was about to dissolve into something infinitely more embarrassing to a man like Bill.

John smiled and nodded, and over John's shoulder he noted that Enid was crying.

Back in John's apartment Jalen was watching a cooking show, which John thought must be like science fiction to the gaunt and scrawny boy, who would always eat like a pig when he was at John's place and, John surmised, nowhere else.

After the friendly rebuff of the Prestons, John found the resolve to do something he was on the fence about since he decided to re-locate. He went to his safe and took out a wooden pistol case and ten boxes of Eley Tenex Pistol .22lr ammunition, assured Jalen of his swift return, and went back to the fourth floor to pay a visit to his friend Judy.

16

Judy's parents despised John completely. Her mother was an alcoholic and hated John because of the gentlemanly attentions he lavished on her daughter. Her father, though, was just a prick. They, too, had not yet evacuated, but were, like most civilians, in the process of gathering their essential effects.

Only the lucky, the wealthy, and the well-connected (no one John knew) had access to commercial trucks and vans. Most other people had to grab what was necessary, hide or secure what they couldn't take in their cars and pickups (if they even had a vehicle of their own), and hope that they would be allowed to return to their homes before the inevitable looters beat them to it. Those that had no transportation were herded into busses, permitted only a coat, a bedroll, and a carry-on each, and driven to the airport near Petoskey where they would stay camped in the hangars until the crisis passed.

John's knock was answered by Judy's father, a small, pockmarked man with a perpetual smirk on his face. "What do you want?"

"Well, since we won't have the pleasure of sharing the same apartment anymore, I thought I'd like to say goodbye to Judy. I have a little present for her." John would have mauled this creep years ago if it were not for his affection for Judy. He kept civility with him so that he could go shooting with his daughter. Once, Judy accompanied John to Nashville for the Masters, which John won. Along with the Olympic Silver Medal, it was his greatest triumph. Judy's father stared at the wooden box in John's hands.

"You think you're a big shit with all them guns don't ya?" Judy's dad was about 55 and the closest thing to a human rodent that John had ever seen. "I ain't impressed with you. That gun shit's illegal, you know? How'd you like to go to jail, huh?"

"May I see Judy please?"

"*May I*," he mocked. "Yes, I guess you *may*."

Judy appeared as her father slinked into the kitchen, where Judy's mom was tearfully trying to decide what to take away in their little station wagon.

"Johneeeey!" she ran and gave him a hug and let him swing her skinny boyish body around once in the hallway.

"Hi darlin'. You getting ready to go?"

"We're going to my uncle's in Detroit," Judy made a face. "Yuck. Where are you going to go?"

"I'm leaving. I'm going up north and I'm not coming back here."

"Well, I already wrote out my new address for you," Judy dug in her jeans' pocket and offered John a scrap of paper. "I don't know how long we're going to be there."

"I know. No one knows that yet."

Judy's father's voice next boomed from the kitchen. "Judy! Tell that bum you got things to do!"

John ignored the slight and gave her the wooden box. "Here darlin'. It's a present."

She opened the lid and gasped. "My God, *it's your Hammerli!*" There, snuggled in the purple velvet was the gun that John won most of his trophies with, a Hammerli 162.

"You could get in a lot of trouble for having this, you know," John said quietly. "If you don't want it, I'll understand."

Her clear blue eyes widened. "Are you crazy? This is officially my coolest possession, *ever!*"

"It might be a little heavy for a skinny girl like you. Remember it'll need a battery soon," he smiled as he noted the glow of delight in Judy's face. "I'm not going to shoot competition anymore." He bent down and collected the ammo from the floor. "This is hard to get," he handed her the bundle. "If I get a line on more I'll let you know."

"JUDY! Goddam it!" her father bellowed.

"I'm coming!" she hollered back.

"If he ever lays a hand on you I'll slit his throat," John said grimly. "Will he give you a problem about the gun?"

"He won't." She giggled. "He leaves me alone. Besides," she poked him in the chest, "he's afraid of you.".

"He should *always* be afraid of me. Tell him if anything happens to that gun he'll deal with me personally, and that means in person." He kissed her on the cheek.

"I need you to tell me that you'll stay in touch with me," Judy whispered.

"I promise."

They hugged one more time, and Judy disappeared behind the closed door. As John made his way back downstairs, he thought of how he would miss Judy. They were never lovers, they were as brother and sister, and she was the only woman he ever knew who was a real friend to him.

The apartment next to him belonged to the Locatelli family, and John knocked at the door to complete his last bit of apartment business. The door swung open to the pretty but beat face of Maggie Locatelli. The four kids in the background were running around and making an incredible racket. Maggie stepped out into the hall.

"Hi Johnny," she said in her Italian accent, which John always enjoyed. When she was upset at her husband Tony she swore in Italian, which was a routine and colorful experience. "Where are you gonna go, eh?"

"Up north, Maggie. I'm not coming back."

"Oh, that's too bad. We'll miss you," she stroked his chin. She liked to touch him when Tony, who was a good buddy to John, wasn't around. "The kids will miss you, but you won't miss the noise, eh?"

"Are you kidding? I'll miss all of you guys. Tony home?"

"No, he's got to take care of some things."

"Listen, Maggie. After I leave, I want you to help yourself to anything in my apartment. If you don't get it, the looters will," John checked himself, too late.

Maggie's brow clouded. "Oh no. Don't say that," Maggie dropped her head. "I dunno what we're goin' to do, Johnny." He, on impulse, reached into his pocket and pulled out the small wad.

"Here's a thousand dollars." He shoved it in her hand. She was dumbstruck. "I owe it to Tony," he lied. "He'll know what it's about. I uh… I didn't want to leave without paying him back."

"What?" Maggie could not understand.

"Gotta go, Maggie." He kissed her on the lips and they embraced. "I'll be in touch," he lied again. Maggie sensed the truth, closed her eyes, lifted her chin, and opened her lips. They kissed again, a real kiss that they both felt in their deepest places. John released her and beheld her with a look of guilt and desire. He turned with a heavy sigh and walked back to his apartment. He dared not look back.

He stood in the middle of his apartment, surveyor of all he owned. Her kiss had unnerved him, and he needed to focus. He made a mental inventory.

AR-15; Colt .45 Pistol, A little bit of match ammo for both; A few rounds of standard ammo for the .45; Mossberg 500 shotgun and a full case of shells; Ek battle knife; Cleaning and maintenance stuff; Gerber multi-tool; A single knapsack of clothes; $9,000 in hundred dollar bills; $84 in other cash.

John turned to Jalen, still dutifully watching television. "Jalen, do you have anything at your place that you want?"

The boy thought a moment. "Not really."

"No teddy bears or toys or anything like that?"

Jalen stared into the TV and shook his head no.

Well, John thought, *that's convenient.* He looked out the window and noticed that the police had made his street one-way to facilitate the heavy traffic flow.

"You ready to boogie, kid?" he asked Jalen as he turned off the old TV that he would definitely not miss.

"Where we going?" Jalen asked eagerly as he sprang from his seat.

Ignoring the question, for now, John burdened Jalen with a few bags to carry and instructed him to take them downstairs. John took his gear, strapped to his body in two large packs, with the jewelry he purloined from Green's house hidden within, with his shotgun cased in one hand and his AR-15 hardcase in the other. All firearms were illegal, but the AR-15 was more illegal than most. It was an excellent defense gun, and John was determined to get it to his car one way or the other.

The unlikely pair made their clumsy way down the street to John's car. The traffic was still pretty fierce, but thinning a bit, John observed. They made their way at last, Jalen huffing and puffing dramatically the last few yards to the car, where he threw down his big packs on the curb with an exaggerated flourish. John chuckled to himself as he opened the trunk and placed the baggage inside. All arranged, he grabbed the AR-15 case and placed it inside. *Everything finally in order,* he thought and reached up to shut the trunk lid.

"Hold it right there, Wheelwright," came a deep voice behind him. Without turning, he knew he would have to confront the one man in town that he would have liked to avoid. "Jalen, get in the car," John said quietly to the boy.

"Stay right there, boy," came the voice again. "Turn around, Wheelwright." John turned.

"Hello, Henry."

Henry was an old school chum. He was a bully, but not toward John, who would not tolerate it. He was one of Oslow's finest, and he stood now in full officer regalia. Today was showtime!

"Isn't it time for your donut break, Henry? I didn't think you'd be walking your usual beat today, what with the evacuation and all." John inquired casually.

"I'll ask the questions," he took a step toward John. "What's in that case?" He pointed to the AR-15 hardcase.

"My saxophone."

"Open it."

John was edgy. Henry unsnapped the thumb release on his holster.

"I said open it," the fat cop barked. "You didn't play the saxophone in high school, and I don't think you play it now."

Henry was instrumental in landing John in jail for the only time in his life. John was drunk one New Year's Eve five years before and was goaded into shooting his shotgun into the air at midnight, and for a few minutes afterward, in joyful, holiday abandon. Classmate Henry showed up in the squad car and chased John on foot for half a mile before he caught him, and then beat him with the help of a fellow peace officer into unconsciousness. John spent the night in jail and the next two days in the county hospital.

"Now you open that goddam case up now, or else I'll open it for you."

John turned and unsnapped the case, pulled back a red velvet liner, and revealed the AR-15.

"Well now," Henry gloated softly. "I'll bet you don't have a Special License for that."

22

"It's right underneath the gun, actually," John said calmly. "I always keep it with the gun."

"Show me," Henry said. "And don't do anything stupid. Just lift it up, get the paper, and let me see it." Henry took out his pistol, a Glock 9mm, and leveled it at John. Reaching down into the trunk John grabbed the rifle by the wrist.

"Hold it there," Henry ordered. "On second thought, I'll take a look. You stand aside."

John grabbed the handguard of the rifle with his other hand, spun quickly and smashed the butt of the gun into Henry's nose, knocking the cop to the ground. John picked up the dazed Henry's pistol and threw it into the trunk, and with a fluid motion knocked Henry quite out with an identical smack to the nose.

"Do 'im!" John heard a hoarse yell. *"Do the pig!"*

John turned, looked high and saw two men, one white and one black, gawking at him out of an upstairs window of one of the boarded-up homes.

"Do the pig, man!"

John dragged Henry to a nearby dumpster and sat him up against it. All the while, little Jalen stood and watched, wide-eyed and excited but not out of control. Henry turned to him. "Time to go, kid. Get in."

John steered the car into the traffic, blended and lost among the others, and was on his way north at last.

3

The pair sped east on Route 68 toward I-75, traffic thinning with every mile they put behind them. Jalen was most curious about their destination, but John was noncommittal, and so lost in his own thoughts that Jalen found him a most unexciting travel companion. He soon fell asleep in the back seat.

It was a beautiful day, but not for driving. John had left his sunglasses back at his apartment and cursed himself for his oversight. He decided to spring for a pair of cheap shades when he stopped for gas, which would have to be soon. It was thoughts of the police that had him preoccupied. The money and the little bit of Mrs. Green's jewelry was troubling him not at all; he was worried about Officer Henry. He could still see him lying against the dumpster, face crimson with blood from his burst nose. Henry knows who did it, has the license plate number, and was crazy enough to continue the grudge match until he found John. Though the police were no longer a terribly effective force in the backwoods, where anarchy and banditry reigned supreme, no one wanted to mess with them. When *they* were mean and murderous, it was *legal*. And weapons violations were high on the list of prosecutions – the kind that took place on the side of the road, when the cops turned their cameras off, confiscated your weapons, and beat the daylights out of you. Most of these weapons were kept or sold by the crooked cops to the highest bidders, and prices were high.

It occurred to John as he sped along the highway that it was gun control that seemed to bring everything to a head. Laws were passed in quick succession over a few short years to limit possession of firearms and, finally, to ban

24

them from civilian hands altogether. At first, compliance with the laws was very low – few turned in their weapons. The politicians claimed that it was a crime issue, that the half-billion firearms in private possession were at the root cause of America's civil decay.

Finally, as Americans began to wake up to the fact that their country had been yanked out from under them, all pretense was dropped, and the government began house-to-house searches and seizures for firearms, ammunition, especially reloading equipment. Terror became an important tool. Though this had the effect of increasing compliance with gun laws, it also created a large, hard, and successful resistance movement. These brave men and women shamed John. But he had awakened and burned the bridges to his old life with a vengeance. He knew his family had to be among the resistors, that they would never give in, and he would join them if they would have him.

Jalen was crying. John looked back and saw that he was asleep but whimpering like a baby. *Christ*, John thought. *That kid has a rough road.*

When the interchange for I-75 was advertised one mile ahead, John decided to stick to the backroads after all, passing through Indian River.

"33 to 23 to the Straits," he said aloud. John reasoned that any search for him would be confined to the area west of I-75, so his tactic was to parallel the freeway a little bit east, all the way up to the Straits of Mackinac. The great bridge that spanned the straits had been badly damaged by, *who?* John wondered. The official news would have it that it was blown by local thugs who just want to make trouble, but even the average idiot had ceased to believe the lies of the official news reports years ago.

The red helmets had been using the bridge to move munitions and *materiel* into the U.P. to bring 'order' to the area and root out armed resistors, to whom they and the official media referred as outlaws and bandits. Whoever blew the bridge did so just enough to disable it and make repairs a difficult and protracted proposition. *Whoever blew the bridge*, John mused, *knew what they were doing.*

John decided to stop for gas and sunglasses (if he could find some) at a little town south of Cheboygan called Philadelphia. *City of Brotherly Love,* John thought to himself. He couldn't dally, not even for a little while, because it was common knowledge that the ferry services at the straits were heavily guarded by a rotating roster of police forces at irregular intervals, and he guessed that his arrival may have been anticipated. John would have to abandon the car and arrive in the U.P. on foot. With his delicate baggage, this could be a dicey situation indeed. He thought of burying the guns and coming back for them when the heat was off.

Philadelphia had one gas station, one bar, a sort-of grocery store, and a vacant lot on the four corners of the center of town, formed by an intersection of two roads which sported a traffic signal in the middle. A few old buildings housing the handful of requisite businesses that a town required radiated from the town's center for a few hundred yards in each direction. It was entirely typical for a tiny northern Michigan hamlet.

John pulled up to the pumps at "Philly Corners," turned off the engine, and considered his situation for a moment. He only needed a couple of gallons of gas, but decided to fill it up anyway in case something went awry.

"I'm hungry, John," came a tired little voice from the backseat. Jalen stretched like a cat and sat up in his seat. "Any food?" He blinked and looked around. "Where are we at?"

"There's a bar across the street," John answered. "We'll see what they've got to scarf down quick. We don't have time to fart around." John got out of the car and worked the pump. Jalen stretched and looked around. Gas dispensed, John went inside to pay the man, and when he emerged saw the tail end of Jalen vanish into the bar across the street. "Oh, shit," John whispered. He climbed back into the Taurus and wheeled the old car into the bar lot, got out, patted his .45, which he was now carrying under his jacket in his belt, and entered the bar. It was dark.

"It gets bright fast," the bright little Jalen exclaimed as John's eyes adjusted from the bright sun to the dark bar. There were five men at two tables, and a bartender, who was so slovenly and dirty that he had to be the owner. "They told me to get out, but I said *you* were comin'," Jalen said confidently. John looked around and noted all eyes were on him. Jalen suddenly pointed at one of the occupied tables and exclaimed, "Chess!"

Jalen ran to the table and stood next to the board. The two men, about 60, each with an empty shotglass and mug of beer in front of them, turned to stare at the boy, then at each other with an I-smell-shit look, and then at John, who stood leaning against the bar. He knew exactly what they were thinking.

"We'll be out of here soon," he told the men. "Just passin' through."

"Good idea, mister. We don't serve kids, and we don't serve coons," the bartender explained and the three younger men at the other table sniggered and drank. "Not even little ones. You gotta draw the line somewhere."

The two chess players turned back to the game, uncomfortable with their little black observer, but willing to endure this uncouth visitation.

"Couple pieces of jerky, couple of boiled eggs, couple of bags of chips," then, remembering Jalen's preference, John said, "Make that barbecued chips." He looked back at the table.

"I resign, I guess," the bearded man said quietly to the other.

"Beat your ass again, eh Buzz?" the other was triumphant, and stretched wide with a yawn that said – *that was that!*

The bold Jalen reached over and moved the black bishop forward.

"What the fuck 'r you doin', you black..." the victor's voice trailed off as he looked at John looking at him.

"Jalen, come over here," John called to the boy.

"But I can win!" he called back. "In four moves I can win!"

"Little nigger got you beat, Sam?" said one of the drunks at the adjacent table, and the others laughed. John gave him a sharp look.

"Here's your order, mister," the bartender said ominously. "$20.25. Pay and hit the road."

John dug into his pockets and called again at the mischievous boy in a slightly louder tone. "Jalen. I said to come over here."

But the vanquished player had risen from his chair and motioned for Jalen to sit. Oh, this was to be good sport for the boys, who could have a laugh no matter what the outcome.

The man called Sam moved his pawn forward to threaten the boy's bishop. Jalen ignored the threat and moved an isolated pawn forward. Sam took the bishop. Jalen moved the pawn again. Sam couldn't believe he was playing chess with a little nigger who kept making stupid moves. He shook his head and took the pawn with his own

28

pawn. Jalen took his other bishop from his back rank, no longer blocked, and moved it out.

"Checkmate!" the happy boy cried out.

The adjacent table was emptied and all gathered round for a look at the chessboard. Sam was bug-eyed. Then ashamed. Then mad. John came forward with his bag of munchies and took the boy's arm. "Let's go. *Now.*" He tugged the little victor out of his chair.

One of the drunks grabbed Jalen's other arm and held him still. "No, stay awhile, Sam needs a few chess lessons." All the men except Sam laughed hysterically. The drunk continued. *"Beat by a nigger boy!"* he howled to the ceiling.

John shoved the man, who slipped on some spilled beer and slid to the floor. John pulled Jalen behind him and pushed him toward the door. All merriment ceased abruptly.

"Get out!" the bartender barked, and John and Jalen backed out of the barroom. They hurried into their car, spinning gravel and impatient to hit the highway.

In his rear-view mirror, he noted that most of the men from the bar had emptied into the parking lot and stood to watch. John had to remind himself to slow down. He speeded when he was angry, and he was steaming: at himself for going to a redneck whiskey joint with a black boy in a shithole town; with the bar scum that called Jalen a nigger and laid hands on him; and at Jalen. He turned to the boy now sitting next to him.

"You little son of a bitch." He was surprised at his own anger. Jalen's head drooped, and he looked sad. "When I tell you to do something, *then god fucking dammit to goddam hell,* YOU DO IT!" He seethed. "I don't know what I'm going to do with you. I don't know. *But as long as you're with me, then I'm in charge of you, and* YOU WILL MIND ME."

Jalen was blubbering quiet tears, now. After barely a minute, John felt himself softening, against his will. "I never saw you cry before, and now here's three times in one day." He took a few deep breaths. "When your aunt left, when you were sleeping, and now this!" he said to the boy, whose sobs continued. John paused to collect himself.

"I know you had a tough day, but I did too," John said to close the subject, having perhaps put too fine a point on it all. "So, let's just stay calm and..." he fished for words, "just relax. Okay?" He looked over at Jalen. "Jesus Christ, don't use your sleeve to wipe your nose."

"I don't cry when I'm asleep."

"Yeah. Right." John handed him a box of tissues from the glovebox. "You're right. Sorry."

A glance in the Ford's rear-view mirror revealed a sight that turned John's guts to water. A late-model Chevy was speeding toward them with a flashing cherry on the roof. A siren began to blare.

"Oh shit," John breathed.

"Cops!" Jalen hollered.

His mind raced. Outrunning the Chevy was out of the question. There were no turn-offs around, this was not John's turf, and that car must have been going well over a hundred. He wanted no more violence against cops but was not willing to be taken back to Oslow, to Officer Henry, and maybe, to the domain of the emperor Green.

He slowed and pulled the car to the side of the road. *He had no plan.*

The big Caprice pulled not behind John's car, but in front of it. Four men emerged, all with shotguns and all pointed at John, who realized, with a strange sense of relief, that these were not cops at all – these were four of the five men from the bar in Philadelphia. The vanquished Sam was not among them. The flashing red cherry atop the Chevy was one of those magnetic stick-on deals.

Two of the men opened fire with shotguns, blowing out all four tires and much of the fender surrounding them. John was ordered out with the boy.

They went about their work with a grim, silent determination, moving next to the trunk while the other two men covered John with their shotguns, with an attitude that permitted no negotiation. Jalen was terrified, but still and quiet as he hugged John tightly.

They opened the trunk and took the suitcase, the bags, the long guns and the cop's pistol. They made no fuss over their booty, they just took it away and loaded it into the capacious trunk of the blue Chevy. They then searched the glove box and passenger area and found nothing of interest. Standing back, the two men reloaded and spent six shots each blasting the holy hell out of John's Taurus, which was now a total wreck. One of the men, the man that John pushed in the bar, opened the engine compartment and ripped away any and all wires visible to him. He nodded to the others.

John thought about the .45 on his hip, but thinking is all he did. These men would have killed him in a second and with the slightest provocation. He put one arm around Jalen and watched as the men got back in the Chevy, turned, and sped away.

John looked at Jalen and smiled. "You can cry again if you want."

The boy shrugged his shoulders and grinned nervously at his new guardian.

Early September nights can be frigid in northern Michigan, particularly so when one is obliged to spend the night sleeping in the woods in one's street clothes. This, thought John, is to be avoided. He took inventory again.

He still had more than $9,000 on him, though almost entirely in hard-to-change and easy-to-track $100 bills. He still had his precious .45, one magazine half-full of home-grown match ammo, and another two magazines of old Remington hollowpoints. He had his wallet and the clothes on his back. And he had little Jalen. He wanted to blame the boy for his troubles, but his heart wasn't in it. He liked the way he beat the redneck at chess. That was a class act. He laughed to himself.

"What's so funny?" Jalen asked, staring up at John. "I'm not crying, but I'm not happy, you know."

"Think about it this way: you're not dead," he answered the boy. "Howdja like to be dead, eh?" He poked Jalen in the ribs and made him laugh.

"We can't drive the car, can we?" Jalen asked, touching a blast hole in the fender.

"Nope. We've got to hitch-hike."

"Cool!" Jalen exclaimed. "Where to?"

"Up north. Let's hope there's some traffic on this road."

They stood in the beautiful sunshine for the better part of an hour with not a single passing car to petition. It would be dark in a couple of hours, John realized. They needed a ride. Jalen had been standing with his thumb out even though there was not a car in sight. He was getting into being a hitchhiker. Practicing, you might say. In this neck of the woods, he needed all the practice he could get, for John feared that a little black boy might repel any potential ride-providers passing through. He was right. In the next hour, four cars passed the duo, never even slowing down.

He sat on the cold pavement next to Jalen, who had finally tired of his hitchhiking pose. The pines smelled sweet. John always liked the eastern half of the northern lower, preferring its rugged, primitive terrain to the more populated and gently rolling hills of the western lower. Here, it was almost like home. About 50 yards away, a flock of turkeys ran across the road noisily, a big tom puffing up and promenading in a noisy circle before disappearing into the swampy jungle.

Another hour passed, and the sun was reddening the sky. Jalen sat on the grass and played with sticks he had gathered. It put John in mind of firewood, and the fact that he had no matches.

"A car." Jalen pointed.

Good, John thought as he noted the growing image and sprang to his feet. *Coming the right way, too.* The last thing he wanted was a ride back toward the City of Brotherly Love.

The car, a big Buick at least 50 years old but beautifully maintained, slowed down and halted majestically in front of the two hitchhikers. The driver, a stubby fellow with white hair and a white beard, and thick horn-rimmed glasses, called out, "All aboard!"

John climbed in front, Jalen in back. It was as comfortable as a livingroom couch, and almost as big. "Nice to get comfortable," the weary John confided to his rescuer, who sped off down the grey ribbon of northbound road.

"Name's Chris," the driver nodded at John.

"I'm John and that little fellow in the back is Jalen."

"Hi," Jalen called through the window breeze.

"That breeze too cold on you, Jalen?" Chris asked.

"I'll just move over," the boy said and scooched over a couple of feet.

"Where you headed?" Chris inquired.

"To the straits, then across."

"Bridge is still out, you know."

"I know."

They drove in silence for a few minutes and Chris put up the windows as the chill moved in and put the lights on. Those old electric windows zipped right up tight.

"Nice car," John wondered aloud at the good shape of the old Detroit iron.

"It's about all I own," Chris said with a yellow-toothy grin. "You know, pardon me but I'm naturally nosey. You got no car, no bags, and a little boy that ain't yours, and you're going across the straits to the U.P. Is that an accurate appraisal?"

John had to laugh. He liked the disarming way of this fellow and felt an urge to confide in him that was hard to stifle, but he managed. "That's about the size of it," John admitted. "How about you? Where are you headed?"

"I drive around the country and write poetry. Michigan mostly. I like Michigan a lot," he turned with a look of mock-horror, "Up here, you understand. Not down south."

"Yeah," John said. "Flint, Detroit, those are bad scenes."

"Gettin' worse, too," Chris assured John. "Lots of red helmets in Detroit now. Suburbs, too. It's like a police state."

John was weary of these awful thoughts and changed the subject. "So, who needs poets these days, anyway?" John was playful.

So was Chris. "You do," he said. "You mean, how do I make my living?"

"Sure."

"I get published in magazines, put a book out every year or two."

"Poetry?" John asked incredulously.

34

"Nah," Chris laughed. "Fiction. Pure pulp. It's comin' back, you know. These here bein' the times that try men's souls and such."

John stared at the poet with a sly smile. Chris looked at him and smiled back in spite of himself. "Also, my brother is a millionaire. He is, shall we say, my greatest patron. My Theo."

"Van Gogh's brother. Kept him alive, right?"

"That's right."

At length, the signs for Mackinaw City began to pop up. They were almost at the straits, and it was quite cloudy and moonless. Jalen was asleep.

"You can't get across tonight, you know," Chris pointed out.

"We'll get a room in town," John stretched and yawned. He had had a somewhat trying day. "What about you?"

"Me too, I guess," the poet answered, and yawned in sympathy.

"Tell you what," John proposed. "I'll buy. I appreciate the lift more than you might imagine. We'll get a nice big motel room. What do you say?"

"I'll buy the drinks. You don't object to a nice bottle of overpriced single-malt Scotch, do you? That'll be my contribution."

"Chris, my poet friend," John grinned, "I do not object."

They laughed quietly together and entered the city limits of that tacky and tasteless little tourist borough known as Mackinaw City.

"Let's do dinner first," Chris suggested as he slowed to legal speed.

John considered. "You know, I'd rather eat in the room. If you don't mind. We can pick something up." He studied Chris. "That okay?"

"Sure, that's okay," Chris agreed. "But I do believe we'll have some interesting conversation tonight." He gave John a sly sidelong glance. John was exhausted, and the thought of rest washed over him like a wave.

There were few vacancies among the motels that night. Though late in the season, there were many travelers who liked to visit the region after the bugs were mostly dead and the tourist-types had gone back to work. They finally found a tawdry little hovel called the Bridgeway Motel and Diner.

Chris got the room (curious as to why his name had to be on the bill), but John picked up the tab, Chris breaking a couple of the $100 bills for him in the process. John stayed in the room while Chris and Jalen tooled about town in search of food and drink.

First stop was the liquor store, where Chris could indulge his favorite vice – single malt Scotches. One of the high points in his life, in more ways than one, was a birthday trip to Scotland financed by his brother. He made a list before he left of all the Scotches that were not imported to America, giving precedence to those distilleries in the string of his visitations.

The selection was adequate, Chris was delighted to discover, and he took a few seconds to ferret out a brew that fit his mood and circumstances. He decided on a 16 year-old Highland Park – a huge, powerful Scotch that seemed to sort well with the sense of adventure that was brewing about his new friend John. Chris added to the bill a six-pack of Guinness, a bag of barbecue chips, and a big plastic bottle of orange soda for Jalen.

That accomplished, they headed for the nearest pizzeria. Jalen got to pick the toppings and, naturally, this required a great deal of consideration. At last, the youth decided that a large pizza with sausage, pepperoni, hamburger, ham, bacon, and double cheese was just about ideal.

Chris stifled a laugh. "Jalen, do you know how greasy that's going to be?" A frown knitted the boy's brow, and the poet felt an instant flash of guilt. "But, hey, let's give it a try anyway, eh?" he said with a smile, and Jalen clapped his hands with excitement.

They waited for the food they chatted about this and that, Chris stifling the urge to probe the boy for the details he longed to know about John and his situation. He thought that to do so would be an unfriendly gesture, and he had no wish to jeopardize what he hoped would be an interesting friendship. In a few minutes, the clerk handed Chris the hot, aromatic box of very meaty pizza, and the two made their way to the big Buick parked out front.

When they returned to the motel they found John out like a light. Chris let him sleep, and he and Jalen drank beer and orange soda, ate incredibly greasy meat pizza, and watched movies on TV. It was a great night. Jalen liked Chris, who not only wasn't mean to him but treated him like a grown-up. Chris liked Jalen, because Chris liked children, particularly bright ones, and because the poet led a lonely life and was warmed by the company. They all were sound asleep by midnight, the bottle of Scotch unopened on the dresser.

4

John was up with the sun and took a long, hot, heavenly shower, particularly pleased with the showerhead, one of those water blasters that can be twisted to give a sort of water-massage. John was a lifelong connoisseur of showers, often incurring his father's wrath as a boy for using up all the hot water at least once a day, usually twice. When he got out he made Jalen, who did not share John's high regard for the shower experience, get in there and do the same. He felt like a dad and didn't really relish the feeling.

Climbing back into very dirty clothes was such a drag that John felt that the sublimity of his shower experience was totally nullified. The only solution was to go into the chic, overpriced downtown of Mackinaw City, mingle with the tourists, and buy some new clothing. He accomplished this while the other two were leisurely getting ready for their day. He also wrote down the sizes on the labels in Jalen's pants, shirt, and jacket, and made a note to buy the next size up, for they were too small for the growing boy.

John returned with a new suit of clothes, plenty of spare clothing in a new knapsack, clothes for Jalen in a knapsack of his own, new jackets and heavier coats for both, the long-desired sunglasses, and the same old wallet about $700 lighter. $100 bills were happily broken in this town, so long as you bought big.

Jalen in his ten years had never once had new clothes, and he was ecstatic. John, who hated putting on clean clothes after dirty ones without an intervening shower, treated himself to a second deluxe deluge in the snazzy motel bathroom.

"You savin' up or catchin' up?" the bemused Chris teased as John emerged from Heavenly Shower II.

"What? Oh, you mean my showers." John pulled on his new underpants and snapped the waistband loudly against his stomach and laughed heartily. *"Goddam, I feel great!"* he exclaimed. Chris and Jalen laughed.

John finished dressing and sat on the bed. "Who's for breakfast?"

They were unanimous that food should be an immediate priority as long as, John stipulated, it was consumed at the motel coffee shop. John locked the room, and Jalen the Wiry and Chris the Portly had a race to the elevator, which the wily Jalen won by a hair.

The diner area was totally generic, but the attentions of an extremely attractive waitress made John think of sex for only the second time in 24 hours – a personal record since puberty. They all ate heartily and slumped into their seats with dreamy smiles, sipping good, fresh coffee – John's hot, black and strong ("Just like my women," he joked), and which Chris took with at least six sugars ("Till it doesn't dissolve anymore,") and lots of cream. The trio sated, the business of the day forced its way into the breakfast cheer as a rude wedge.

The barges were beginning to fill, and the ferry services were processing the crowds of people who were hoping to make the crossing into the Upper Peninsula with as little hassle and delay as possible. "Nice meeting you, Chris," John said finally, "but it's time for us to take our chances at the ferry."

Chris put his feet up on the booth and waxed philosophical. "You know, when you do what I do, you develop a good sense of what's interesting and what's not. Know what I mean?" He looked at John. Jalen was squirming and bored.

"Nope."

Chris took off his thick horn-rims and began to polish the lenses with a clean napkin. "I need inspiration. I'm bored. We spent the good part of a day together, and there's a mystery here that really interests me." He replaced the glasses on his bushy, grey head. "I'll take you where you're goin'. We could have some fun. Hell, we didn't even touch the Scotch."

"I'm going about 100 miles into the U.P.," John explained quietly. "We're fleeing that chemical plant bombing, but I had a little trouble with the law on the way out." He explained no more than this.

Chris thought about this for a few moments. "I know people," The poet sat straight up and looked intense. "You're not a bad person. Let's hit the road. We can have some fun."

"Do you understand that if I get busted, you could get busted, too?"

Chris paused now to consider this pearl of logic. "It's worth a try," he concluded with a nod. "Consider me well-advised."

John turned to the fidgety Jalen. "You ready to go?"

"I've *been* ready to go for about *five hours*," he moaned comically.

The trio paid their bill, and John tipped the comely waitress generously for reminding him of the pleasures of the fair sex awaiting him when the heat was off. Her name tag said 'KAREN', and John thanked her personally.

She bestowed a sweet smile on John and said, "I got a break in about ten minutes."

Chris chuckled, and John was embarrassed. He met Karen's pretty eyes and motioned to his two companions. "Some other time, perhaps, hey love?"

40

She laughed and winked at John. "Maybe," she said. John's eye followed appraisingly as she strolled back to the kitchen.

Bags packed, and key returned, the three made their way into the splendid sunshine and down to the majestic Buick. "Let's put the bags in the trunk," Chris suggested.

"Let's keep them on us," John countered. "In fact," John pulled a new pack from within his full pack. "This is for you."

Chris was a little confused. "Why?"

"In case there's a problem, keep what's important to you in your grasp. At least until we clear the straits."

The poet was uneasy, as if the potential hazards of the situation were finally dawning upon him. "Listen," John said. "If you want to part company, I'll understand."

"Do you want my company?" he asked John, who was taken aback by the question.

"Yes," John was almost confessional. "I do. I think it would be fun."

The poet opened his trunk and began packing the bag with the most essential of his essentials. John was expecting to see a stack of notebooks, but instead saw Chris pull out a pricey, slim laptop computer and a few accessories. "Everything I've ever written is on this thing, and backed up plenty," the poet bragged, "so it won't matter if it gets... you know... *lost.*" To this, Chris added clothing and a few effects.

They were soon on their way to the docks and in line waiting for the next barge. John was apprehensive. He had observed police from many services milling about the dock area – state, city, bridge cops, even some red-helmeted soldiers who looked of the Japanese persuasion – Flavor of the Month. Depending upon the nature of the operation, the National Police sometimes avoided the use of native troops in their strategies because they would be less likely to obey shoot-to-kill orders on their own countrymen.

A neat system, John wondered, and shook his head in disgust. Their conquest, however, was far from complete. There were literally hundreds of pockets of resistors nation-wide, many of whom (like the loosely-formed militia in the western Upper Peninsula) were quite successful in living within their own economy and protecting their own. The National Police were spread too thinly, and plainly had their problems. They were also incredibly, comically, inept. Their soldiers were poorly trained, and their 'leadership' was the butt of many jokes and stories.

A man from the bridge authority appeared at the driver-side window. "Morning sir. $25 please."

Chris paid the man, who handed him a receipt, scribbled a code on his windshield with a soap pencil and moved to the next car in line. *So far, so good*, John thought.

They were soon in sight of the barge entrance when John noted with alarm that they were asking for identification – a highly irregular procedure. Chris noticed, too, and looked back at John with an alarmed look. John shrugged it off and winked at Chris, who was not fooled by his new friend's casual attitude. There was no way out of the line. They had to see it through.

The man asking for ID was not a cop, but a bridge authority officer. He stuck his head in the driver window and looked inside. "Identification, please." He said as he scanned the faces inside. His glance paused on John and went back and forth from him to Jalen. *He knows*, John stiffened at the thought. He was quick. In lieu of his ID, he handed the officer a piece of paper. The man took it from John's hand carefully and read the note.

"I beat up a cop who had a grudge against me and threatened to kill me. I'm not a criminal. I have no record. Here is $1,000. I will give you $1,000 more when we get to the other side. Please let us pass. I am a patriot."

The man paused and thought. He looked at John and asked, "Are you an X-man?"

All John could think of were the comic book characters, and he wondered what in the hell this guy was talking about. "No," he replied. "I'm not. You mean like the comic books?"

The bridge cop took a long look at John and the boy, put the note and its contents in his pocket and waved the car in to be packed, sardine-like, into the barge. After sweating blood in silence for another half-hour, the bridge man closed the gate and in seconds the barge shoved off, bounding not-too-gently in the waves of the Mackinac Straits. Passage was uneventful. After docking, the cars began the orderly process of deboarding. The same bridge man approached Chris' car.

He looked inside, and John handed him another note. He pocketed the cash without counting it and read the paper.

"Thanks. I'll remember you."

The bridge man looked at John again, a hard look this time, searching in John's eyes for some justification for what he, the bridge cop, was doing.

"Forget me," the bridge officer said quietly. John kept his stare until the man pulled his head away.

The bridge cop waved the car ahead, and the trio snaked their way through the makeshift two-tracks onto Route 2, filled with relief and good cheer, they sped along the spectacular north shore of Lake Michigan toward the farm of John's father and the realm of his childhood friends.

With a couple of miles of highway safely between the Chrismobile and the bridge authorities, Chris could politely contain himself no longer and turned to John, who was serene and positively limp with relaxation.

"Remember me telling you last night that I was kind of a nosey person?"

"Yeah," John recalled with an easy grin. "I remember."

"Well, not that you owe me or anything," the poet fished about for words, "but, you know..."

"What?"

Chris was exasperated. *"Whaddaya mean* 'What?' *What's going on?"* he cried. "I mean, what did you give to the bridge guy back there. For starters."

John laughed and decided to tell Chris the whole sordid tale; from the evacuation announcement, through the Green robbery, taking on Jalen, his bashing of Officer Henry, the bar scene chess game fiasco, and the raid and robbery which followed, to the bribery scenario at the bridge. John was amazed at himself while he told the tale. He had never done anything like that before and had even nurtured a ridiculous pride in his clean record with the authorities.

"I just got fed up and felt like I had nothing to lose, so I settled accounts with some people who were causing a lot of good people a lot of unpleasantness over the years, and I feel ..." John paused for the right word. "... great."

Chris was shocked into silence and remained that way for the next half hour, and John wondered if he did the right thing by leveling with him. He figured he owed him an explanation, for the poet may very well have saved his, and Jalen's, life. He noticed Chris' brow working as if he were having an argument with himself. He was.

Finally, he looked over at John with a sober and serious face. "Okay," he said as if he had thought it all over, and it was alright.

John smiled at the old bard. "And I want to thank you for helping us out," he said with a little formality, which he guessed that Chris would appreciate. "I hope I can return the favor one day." Chris looked over at John for a moment, nodded, and they drove for another few miles in silence.

It is amazing how the terrain, the entire geology, seems to change north of the Straits. John loved the land of his youth, but he never thought the Upper Peninsula was beautiful. It is rocky, sandy, craggy and spectacular, but not beautiful like lower Michigan. There is a gentleness about the lower that the U.P. does not partake in. There is a sense of isolation here that isn't illusory. Here, one can walk for 50 miles without cutting a road; here, the weather can kill you without warning. A bald eagle wafted high above them, suspended motionless in a strong updraft. John pointed the magnificent bird out to Chris and Jalen and took it to his own heart as a good omen. It was good to be back.

"We're going to a little town north of Seney called Fox River," John disclosed at length. "We stay on this till we come to 77. Then head north." He looked over at Chris, who nodded acknowledgment.

About an hour into their cruise, a car came into view on the roadside, under a stand of birch trees, where a young woman was looking under the hood. The ever-helpful Chris wheeled the big Buick over behind the woman's car, and he and John got out to see if they could be of some assistance.

"Howdy," John called to the trim and pretty pair of blue jeans, all that was visible of the busy woman under the hood of the old Ford pickup.

"Just a second," she called back in a strained voice. "Dammit!" She yelled, then slowly extracted herself from the engine compartment and straightening up, turned toward Chris. "Hello."

"Can we help you?" Chris asked the young woman.

"Oh, I hope so. But probably not." She kicked the tire in mock attack. "This old piece of junk." She turned to the sound of John's laughter.

"Oh!" John breathed deep at the sight of the woman and recovered not quite quickly enough to hide his dazzlement. "Hi."

She smiled at his clumsiness, happy at herself for the spell she could still cast over a strong and good-looking man. "I'm Grace," she said.

John nodded. "Hi."

"You said that already," she laughed. "What's your name?"

"Oh yeah, heh," he said cleverly. "John. I'm John. And this here's Chris. And, um, Jalen is in the car."

O damn, she thought to herself. "So, who's Jalen?"

"Oh, he's my a..." what was Jalen exactly? "He's my little buddy."

"Oh good!" Grace yipped, and blushed – her turn to feel clumsy. The two stared at one another nervously but neither could pull their glance away from the other.

Chris was amused. The old poet knew *L'Amour* when he saw it. He was visited many times by the magic himself as a young man and wrote poems about it now. *They're already in love*, he perceived with a smile. "So, um," Chris cleared his throat and peeked into the engine

46

compartment. "What's the matter with your truck, do you think?"

The spell broken, Grace looked sourly at Chris, then at the engine, then gave a big sigh, which John thought was an incredibly beautiful sound. "Transmission," she said. "It's dead. To hell with it." She looked at John. "I wonder if you can give me a lift back to my house?" she asked, wincing a bit. "I live in Newberry."

"Hell yes! No problem!" the helpful John replied without hesitation. Then, remembering his place, he looked over at Chris, who wore, John thought, a most bemused look.

"John's right," Chris confirmed to the relieved young woman. "No problem at all."

"It's on the way. We'll just take 117 straight up," John said enthusiastically as he ushered Grace to the car and opened the back door for her. "Jalen," John called at the lad who had been waiting patiently in the back seat. "This here is Grace. How 'bout you getting into the front seat with Chris."

Hellos said, and everyone settled in, the big Buick sped off again down US-2 toward the turnoff. Grace had perfume on, John noticed. It was so soft and subtle that he thought he might have been imagining the delicate scent of the woman, or maybe flowers from out the window. *Wow*, he thought. *Maybe she just smells that way.* Grace looked at him and smiled, holding his eyes again to her own. John looked away, staring into the grey curls of the back of Chris' head. *Not quite the same*, he thought to himself with a stupid smile.

Grace, it was revealed in the conversation which followed, was a widow. At this news, John was both elated and ashamed at his elation. He guessed her age at about 30, but her body was so youthful that only the small lines about her blue eyes suggested that she would never see her 20s again. Her husband had been killed by poachers who had been overrunning their small farm for weeks in reckless and greedy pursuit of what little easily-obtainable game remained in the area. He had confronted them and was murdered. John reminded himself that there was no real law in this territory. It was hard to tell the resistors from the brigands and thieves that roamed, pretty much at will, the evergreen jungles of the Upper Peninsula.

John asked what had become of her after her husband's murder, but she declined to answer, she smiled, looked away, and after a few uncomfortable seconds, asked John about himself. He wanted to tell her about what had happened to him in the past few days, but held back, sharing with her a few mundane details, and rather expertly (so he thought) piquing her curiosity for more.

The farm on which Grace lived was small, near town, and with a few neighbor farms close about. It was hard to tell how far back the land was hers, but there seemed to be about 10 acres of crops that had just been harvested and another 20 or so that were bordered by outbuildings, a small orchard, and a couple of old rusting cars. There was also a small lake on the north side, which was probably a border to the next property.

The four travelers got out of the car and John took a deep breath. "Wow, it's warmed up some," he noted. The temperature must have risen to about 80 in the past couple of hours. It was a lovely September day in the U.P.

"I'll make lunch," Grace called at her doorstep to the others. "You can all come in if you want." The boys took her up on that suggestion. Upon entering, it became evident that this was a lady's house. All of the effects were feminine, and everything was spotlessly clean. There were flowers everywhere.

"I grow them," she said to Chris, who went from vase to vase like some tubby mutant grey honeybee, sniffing heartily at each display. John liked the flowers, too, kept his eyes peeled for some sign of a male presence, which he did not find, except for a picture on the fireplace of her late husband. Grace busied herself at making lunch, and she was very happy with the idea of feeding these hungry fellows. She liked them all very much and was curious about Jalen. *How in the world did those fellows come together?* she wondered as she mixed the salad dressing into the tuna and onions.

The three congregated in the large living room of the otherwise small farmhouse. There was no totally comfortable place to lie, or even sit down, Chris and John both noted privately. It seemed Grace had a decorous streak in her. The two men squeezed into a couple of straight-backed chairs, while Jalen sat on the floor, playing with the Swiss Army knife John had given him. In a few minutes, Grace entered with a plate stacked high with toasted sandwich halves. She went back for a second trip and returned with two Budweisers and two cans of 7-Up. Watching the hungry crew dive into their lunch, Grace slipped upstairs almost unnoticed.

Lunch was good.

"Mmmm. Wonner 'ere Grace went, ummm?" Chris inquired through his overstuffed mouth. He helped slide the bolus into his belly with a copious gulp of Bud.

John winced at Chris and was glad that Grace wasn't in the room to witness his inelegant new friend tie on the feedbag. Jalen nibbled at a sandwich half and sipped at the soda. John wasn't too hungry, but dutifully ate one of the sandwiches. The Budweiser, however, disappeared in two long gulps. Almost on cue, Grace entered with more beers.

She had changed clothes and stood radiant and smiling before the admiring trio of well-fed males.

"God, you look beautiful," John said aloud and without calculation – he was hardly aware of the words. It was as if they were drawn out of him. It wasn't his style to complement women that he hardly knew; he always thought they should earn it, but he said this with such honest regard that he made Grace blush for the second time that day – not an experience she often had.

"Thank you," she whispered as she distributed the beers and sat next to the happy Chris, who was now working on his fifth sandwich half, his mustache and beard astrew with crumbs.

John grabbed another sandwich to occupy his hands while the four chatted quietly. Whenever he could, and without rudely coming across as the leering lecher he was gleefully becoming, John would steal long looks at Grace. She had put on a soft, red, wrap-around skirt that came just below her knees and rode up just above them as she sat. Her calves were smooth and creamy white against the skirt, and she was barefoot. She wore no nail polish, but her feet were slim and well-scrubbed. She wore a white lace top and no jewelry of any kind. She needed no ornament.

Grace was having fun looking back at John when she thought that he didn't expect it, catching him leering at her. She had not played this game in years, and it made her tingle with an old excitement. Sometimes she would look away and engage Chris in long stretches of conversation, which she would not recall, and which served only to allow John to take her in through his eyes in long adoring looks. She let him devour her this way.

They talked for three hours, small talk mostly, and it was now late afternoon. Grace, it was revealed, only rented the farm. She was forced to sell it soon after her husband died. She agreed to vacate the property in three years and paid no lease during this time. She had three months to go.

John and Chris talked about growing up and were armed with numerous and amusing anecdotes which kept the mood light and rolling throughout the afternoon. Jalen, streetwise and sharp as the knife that still fascinated him, laughed at most of the jokes. Grace, who had not laughed so much in her life, reluctantly stood to take leave of the group.

"I've got chores to do that I've been putting off all day," she said with a mock-sad smile. John eagerly, and the lazy Chris reluctantly, volunteered to help with the farm doings. They worked together until after sunset.

John and Chris took turns in the shower while Grace made dinner for them all. Though the showerhead was nothing so glorious as the one in the motel, the very thought that Grace stood naked where he stood now made it a most memorable shower nonetheless. The soap smelled like Grace, and he put the bar under his nose and inhaled eagerly. "Wow," he said aloud. He was sporting quite an erection by this time and wanted to masturbate, but thought better of it. He liked the sexual tension he was feeling in the house of the lovely Grace. He dried off, changed clothes, and joined the trio waiting downstairs for a home-cooked supper.

Grace had slaved over dinner as she hadn't done since holiday meals during her married days, though she was nonchalant, as if it were no big deal. She had killed two hens which she fried up expertly and to perfection. With this, she served a complex herb salad fresh from her garden. She also did subtle and colorful things with sweet potatoes, peas, and carrots that were simple and elegant. With this dinner, she served two white wines, both French, a late model vintage Muscadet and a fine Chablis, obtained from her cellar. Her husband had been a modest but skillful collector. Jalen just ate chicken, but lots of it, and he was having as much fun as everyone else.

Curious it was, John mused while feasting heartily, that Grace had not showered after the hard work. She had worn light coveralls and had slipped back into her previous outfit for dinner. Her hair was tied back, but there were small suggestions of dirt on her face and neck and sweat had curled the small loose hairs near the back of her neck. She looked beautiful even now.

By the time dessert was finished, a simple batch of cookies served with a rich Michigan late-harvest Riesling, it was almost 9 pm. They moved out on the screened porch for a nightcap, which featured some of the Scotch that Chris bought in Mackinaw City, and in which Grace chose not to indulge.

The warmth had not disappeared as it so often does in the fall northern nights, but it had become rather humid. The sky was clear, and the moon was one day before full. They talked about everything, and it felt to Grace as though they had known one another for years. They all shared in this great contentment, like a family together, and Grace realized that this was what she wanted, and what she had so terribly missed. She secretly wiped away a slightly inebriated tear.

Three sleeping bags had been arranged by Grace in the big living room, and when it was time for bed, Grace tucked Jalen in snugly and could not help giving him a goodnight kiss on the forehead, but she declined to offer similar favors to her two grown-up guests. John was filled with affection for Grace and dreaded the morning when they would depart. If Grace felt the same way, John could detect no evidence. He resigned himself to the next day and settled down with his friends to sleep.

John awoke suddenly from a dream in which a donkey was caught in a woodchipper! Earsplitting noises of horrible agony issuing from the great tortured beast as it was sluggishly being ground to death. John was relieved to be awakened from the dream -- but the noise was barely abated. For the room reverberated with the explosive, rasping, and discordant snoring noises of Chris. John had never heard snoring so hideous.

Sleep was not possible in these circumstances, and John's sleeping bag was becoming too warm for comfort. He unzipped the side and stuck out his legs, stretching and waving them in the slightly cooler air of the room. He heard flute music. First, he thought he was imagining it, then that it was a radio, but it was coming from outside, and it was very fine. He closed his eyes and saw Grace, and teetered on the edge of wakefulness, holding tightly to her image in hopes of bringing her with him into his dreams. But alas, the violent snoring of his friend was unlessened, and kept John reluctantly in the land of the wakeful.

The stairway gave a creek, and John heard small, careful footsteps padding down the steps. He looked at the clock, visible just barely in the moonlight, which read 2:30. Grace appeared in the doorway. "John?" she whispered.

"Hi," John sat up.

"Come with me."

He obediently extracted himself from the sleeping bag, fully-clothed, and followed Grace quietly to the backdoor of the house. She had on a long blue robe, cinched tightly at her waist, and she carried an empty bucket covered with a white towel. "Follow me," she whispered.

They stepped into the rich moonlit night, and into the flute song which floated in the air from a nearby farm.

53

They walked toward the small lake which bordered the north side of the property. Grace stopped and turned.

"That's Mr. Ohlsson," she said in a soft voice. "He's very old. He used to be a hippy. Remember them?" They both sniggered quietly. "He likes to smoke pot and drink beer, and on nights like this, he plays his flute. It's a *Japanese* flute."

They listened for a few moments to the magic sound. "Nobody ever complains because he's so incredibly good. I mean… *listen* to this…"

When they reached the sandy banks of the little lake Grace put the bucket down a few feet away and turned to John. She was very nervous.

"It's very beautiful out here," John whispered to the radiant Grace. "Very beautiful." She drew a long breath and tugged slowly at the strand that cinched her waist. Her robe parted. She exhaled slowly, and with a quick, graceful move, the robe fell to her ankles, and she stood before John naked in the silver light of a full moon. She stepped out of the robe, took a single small step toward him, and stood still as a statue.

John wondered if he had indeed taken this goddess into his dream with him, after all. She closed her eyes and waited. John glided to her form, put his hands on her shoulders, and touched his lips to hers. She opened her eyes and pulled back ever so slightly. "No," she whispered. "No kissing. Not yet." She took a backward step. "Just touch me." She closed her eyes again, letting John take in her image, as she knew he longed to do.

Her breasts, John saw, were larger than they appeared when Grace was dressed. In the moon's cool glimmer her nipples cast long shadows all the way across her breasts. John reached out and with thumbs and forefingers, softly squeezed her nipples and rolled them slightly. Grace moaned softly and dropped her head forward, spilling her hair over her shoulders. After a moment, John released his pinching caress and saw her nipples slowly grow erect. He caressed the twin apples of her breasts and marveled at their softness. He let his hand run softly down her stomach and over her hips. Grace lost her balance a bit in a swoon, recovered quickly, leaned over to pick up the towel off the bucket and removed a couple of items from within.

"Here," she instructed softly. "Go into the pond and fill the bucket."

As one hypnotized, he did as he was bid. When he returned, she held out to him a cake of soap and a washcloth. "Give me my bath now," she whispered.

The enchanted John soaked the washcloth and lathered it with the soap, which he tossed beside the bucket. He rubbed her neck and chest with the soapy rag, and then lathered both graceful arms. With bent elbows, Grace held her hands in front of her, palms upturned. John gently lathered every finger in a gentle, soapy massage. Grace was smiling. He returned to the bucket for more water and soap for this luckiest of washcloths.

He lathered next her breasts, and he did this with infinite care, still marveling at the texture and sensation of her nakedness, her nipples still hard and stiff. Next her belly, and then, in languid approach, the soft hair down below. She moaned at this gesture and slightly spread her legs to ease his access into this infinitely fascinating place, moving her bare feet a few more inches apart in the cool sand. John thought it crude to dally here, and daring not to break the spell, moved to her thighs, the muscles of which spasmed ever so slightly in her excitement. At the knees, John returned to the bucket for a reload of water and soap.

He returned quickly to attend to Grace's calves, feet, and then, one by one, her long, thin, toes. He separated each one from its pretty peers and gave it a gentle, soapy, massage. When he finished the last toe, he raised the foot a tiny bit and gave it a little kiss, looking up at Grace who opened her eyes and frowned down at her attendant. "John," she whispered, "don't. No kissing. Not yet."

When he returned from the bucket with a fresh load of water and soap, Grace had turned her back to him and was waiting patiently. Filled with as much admiration for her at this angle as at the former, he lathered her graceful shoulders and spent a long time on her smooth back, Grace purring kitten-like. John then knelt in the sand and paused to run his open palms over Grace's smooth, round bottom. She had stopped purring now, in fact she was not even breathing. Feeling especially naughty, Grace bent forward ever so slowly. John was almost overcome at the endless eroticism of this woman and sighed audibly. Her lovely bottom was wet and streaked with soap running from her back in silverwhite rivulets. He continued to explore her as she bent forward until her hair touched the sand. After a few moments, and with supreme discipline, he picked up the soapy rag and repeated the gestures that his bare hand had made moments before.

With an excitement matched only by his restraint, he finished his appointed task. There now. The goddess had her bath.

Grace straightened gracefully and turned to look at John. They had not looked into one another's eyes since Grace had dropped her robe in the sand. She smiled and turned and walked into the pond, dived almost noiselessly into the water, washing her face, and rinsing the soap from her body. That finished, Grace drifted back to the beach, shivered a bit in the chill, and put her robe back on. As she cinched the cord to her waist, she walked noiselessly to John and kissed him on the cheek.

"Thank you," she whispered, "for my bath." And she walked through the moonlight back toward her house. She paused on the steps and turned to look at the moon. Then at John.

"Good night," she called sweetly and disappeared into the darkness of the house.

John and Grace both lay awake through the remainder of that night. Grace obsessed about the next day; John, after relieving himself in joyless masturbation, tried to get some sleep, but the snoring of his friend Chris was outrageous, and deprived him of any hope of rest. Jalen slept like a log.

At sunrise, Grace hurried outside to do some chores around the farm, and John dragged himself into the kitchen to make some coffee. Chris popped up as if on cue the moment the coffee was finished, totally refreshed after a sound, a very sound, night's rest. Jalen slept peacefully still.

"Mornin'!" the cheerful Chris called to John and poured himself a cup of coffee, banging cupboard doors around searching for the sugar.

John pulled up a chair to the kitchen table and sat, looking cross. "Mornin'," John mumbled in response.

Chris joined him at the table, pausing, as usual, to smell the roses on the way. "Aren't these flowers incredible?" Chris wondered aloud. "Man, that lady sure is somethin', isn't she?" Chris slurped his coffee noisily. John shot him a nasty look.

"Listen, would you mind driving today?" Chris asked his sleepy friend. "I gotta write some."

"No problem."

"You don't look too chipper today," Chris noted. "You feeling okay?"

"You snore."

"I what?" Chris was a little surprised.

"No. You don't just *snore*. You… you…" he thought of the donkey-dream.

Chris looked ashamed. "I'm sorry. I kept you awake."

John glanced up at Chris and sighed. "Ah, that's all right." He tried to smile. "It wasn't all you, I guess." He gulped at the hot java.

The poet snugged his chair up to John's with a conspiratorial gesture. "So," he said quietly, "You stuck on Grace, eh?"

John put his coffee down and stared hard at Chris, who moved his chair back again. "Sorry," he pretended fear and contrition. "None o' my business." John had to laugh at his friend's antics despite his own situation.

It was going to be a cloudy day. It was turning cooler, too. They finished their coffee in silence. It would not have occurred to Chris, but John thought about helping Grace do the chores, but before he could decide, he saw her come into view from behind the large barn. He shook his head.

She came through the door with a gracious smile for all. "Good morning, guys!" she put down the bucket, the famous bucket, in the kitchen corner and turned to her guests. "Whew! I need a shower."

"I thought you liked baths," John said innocently.

Grace gave him her best 'why, what*ever* do you mean?' look and went upstairs to clean up.

"Baths, eh?" Chris said idly.

"Yeah." John sighed and stared across the harvested field. "Baths."

Jalen jumped into the room and yelled *"Boo!"* scaring hell out of both the men. *"Jesus Christ, Jalen!"* John yelled. Jalen cackled gleefully and ran back into the living room.

"Awake now?" Chris chuckled at his friend, who nodded and smiled a resigned smile.

Everyone washed up and changed clothes. John had stopped shaving since leaving town, and his beard was a stubble. *The worst stage,* he thought to himself as he looked in the mirror. The trio gathered up their things and packed the Chrismobile. At the late stages of this process, Grace descended the stairs. John walked in the back door at the same time, looked up and gasped. "God. Grace, you look absolutely beautiful. Again."

She had put on a dress of blue and white, something that a teenage girl might wear to church on a special occasion, and put her thick black hair up, a few elegant twists held together with a couple of long, black wooden sticks that had garnets on the end of them. Grace looked resplendent in this outfit, like it was designed for her. But her face was strained with emotion. "You're leaving now?" she asked softly.

"Well, we gotta get going, yeah." John looked away, and they stood in silence for a whole minute. John climbed the stairway to the step under Grace's. They were the same height now.

"Grace."

She looked into his eyes and brushed a tear away from her own. "What, my dear?"

"Will you come with me?" he whispered.

Grace closed her eyes, tilted her face up, and parted her lips. John kissed her. Finally.

"Yes," she whispered. "I'll go with you." She smiled, and the two embraced.

"She comin'?"

The two lovers looked down the stairway at little Jalen, mischievous in his interruption of their loveplay.

"Yeah, she's coming," John answered the boy. "That alright with you?"

"Sure is!" he yelled gleefully and bolted out the screen door to tell Chris.

"You could stay here with me, you know," Grace leaned her cheek against John's.

"That's a possibility," John answered. "Come with me today to Fox River and meet my family. We'll hang there for a while. They've got a lot of room." John laughed. "You'll like my sister. And my dad and brother."

"Are they X-men?" Grace asked. John pulled back as if stung.

"What's X-men?"

"X," she couldn't believe John didn't know. "X is the real law around here. If you can call him that," she grimaced. "Most folks hate him, but he runs things. He's a terrible bully, but only if you get in his way. He keeps the red helmets on their toes, and the local law, they don't mess with him. He's dangerous. If your brothers aren't X-men, then, I don't know..."

"I'll tell you right now, they're not." John began to feel concern for his family, a fiercely independent bunch, and guilt at losing touch with them for so long. His father particularly was not the type to be bullied. By anyone.

"The guy at the bridge asked me if I was an X-man." John looked at Grace, a hard look, full of doubts. "You know, you don't really know me very well. You might not approve of, well..."

"I'll approve." She kissed his cheek and beamed him a sweet smile. "Listen. I've got to go to the Ohlssons and ask if they'll watch the farm for a few days." She paused to think. "I want to get some wine from the cellar to take along..." She looked up at John with a smile. "And that ought to do it!"

"Don't you need to pack clothes and stuff?"

"John, my dear," she gave him a sweet/wicked smile. "I'm already packed!" she said and twisted away from him with a giggle, sprinted out the door, and ran barefoot all the way to the Ohlsson farm.

An hour later the happy quartet was speeding toward Fox River Village. They had taken on an extra suitcase and a case of some of the excellent wine that Grace had cellared. John was driving, and Chris was in the back seat typing furiously on a new *magnum opus*. Jalen would become very interested in Chris' laptop computer, which had a chess program. Chris, wanting a little peace, had not yet told the enthusiastic Jalen about this feature.

John had decided to stop by his uncle Ty's house in Seney before moving on to his dad's place. Ty was the older brother of John's mother. He was in a wheelchair since the accident that killed John's mother ten years before. He was the driver, hit head-on by a drunk in an April fog on Highway 77. John's father, though always civil to Ty, had never forgiven him for being the driver of the car that took his wife away. John had never blamed Ty, whom he knew was not at fault. That accident devastated Ty, but he tried to keep his spirits up with his watercolor paintings, and his bills paid by speculation in the stock market. He was pretty good on both counts.

As John wheeled the Chrismobile into the long asphalt driveway, he was happy to see that Ty's house looked just like he remembered it from six years ago. Ty paid local folks to keep up the landscaping and help him with his domestic efforts. He always employed pretty agency women for this latter task, but it was Ty's habit to drink heavily on occasion and to try to bed these young ladies. (Only Ty's legs were disabled.) The girls wanted to complain, and some did, but work was always scarce in the U.P., and they tried to stick it out as long as they could. Some, rumor had it, even succumbed to Ty's elusive charms. His money, most reasoned, was a powerful aphrodisiac.

John sprang from the car and ran up to the porch, where he was greeted by Ty's big Irish Wolfhound, Chumley, who licked John's hands, wagged his tail, and barked playfully. Ty wheeled into the screened-in porch.

"Hey Ty, some watchdog you got here," John called, fending off the playful Chumley.

"Johnny?" Ty was disbelieving of his own eyes. *"Jesus Christ, it's Johnny!"* he shouted. "Come on in!"

He sprinted up the ramp and bent to embrace his uncle, who hugged him to his muscled chest with huge, strong arms. John felt an unexpected flood of emotion as he held his uncle. Ty released him suddenly, and John stepped back, blinking away a tear.

"Goddam, Johnny boy, you look great," Ty said. "Who's out there?" he gestured to the car.

"Friends."

"Bring 'em in." Ty spun the chair about and wheeled into the big house.

John waved at the three to come inside. He introduced Chris and Jalen. Chris, Ty could understand, but Jalen had him confused.

"Howdy there, little fella," Ty said with a handshake. He looked at John quizzically. "Johnny, how did you come to know this little guy?"

"He's an old friend," he patted the boy's head, a gesture that Jalen hated but tolerated with a scowl. "He lost his family. I took him with me."

Ty shrugged. "What the hell." He looked at Grace, who shucked her elegant beau-catching dress in favor of more practical blue jeans and a man's workshirt. "And who, my lovely, are you?"

"This is Grace," John replied for the smiling woman. "I like her a lot."

"Yeah, I'll bet." Ty pressed her hand and bowed his head. "A pleasure to meet you." He became serious and polite. "Listen, Grace, umm. You know a crippled fellow like me needs some help around the house now and again. How 'bout you..."

John rolled up a nearby Wall Street Journal and began beating his uncle on the head and shoulders as he might an unruly dog. "Stay away from my girl, you old perv!" he yelled. Everyone laughed heartily except Grace, who was a little confused. It was sure good, John thought, to see Tyrone again.

Soon the smalltalk died down and everyone was settled with a favorite drink and some smoked ham sandwiches that his current domestic helper prepared for them. Her name was Jean, and she was quite a departure from the tradition of pretty young things. She was late-middle-aged and quite, umm, *sturdy* looking to say the least, but charming, and always smiling.

"Everybody all set with lunch?" Jean asked the assembly. She looked over at Chris' empty glass. "How 'bout another beer for you?"

"Definitely," was the word Chris attempted to mumble with a mouth full of smoked ham. "Please."

John leaned over to whisper at Ty. "Hell, she's old enough to be your wife."

"Yeah, well, I've settled down a bit," he smacked Jean on the rump as she walked by with a tray of empty plates.

"Stop that, you old pig," she snapped and laughed in spite of herself.

"Fact is, I like her a lot." Ty was earnest. "She stays with me." Ty took a long drink of his home-brew beer, which was dark, strong, and very good, and wiped his chin with the back of his hairy hand. "So. You heard about the trouble and came to see your dad, eh?"

John's smile disappeared, and he studied his uncle's face. "It's pretty much a coincidence that I'm here, Ty. That bombing at the chemical plant down south set me travelin'." John was tense. "Now what trouble are you talking about? Are they okay?"

"It's that bastard X." Ty leaned forward and eyed John coldly. "He's one mean son of a bitch."

Grace went to John's side and put her hand about his waist.

"I asked if they were alright, Ty."

"Sure, physically they're fine. For now. But they can't get work. They won't play the game."

"What's the game?"

"Your dad and Alan and Andrea all lost their jobs because your dad won't cede a piece of land to X. In one day, all three of them were fired from jobs in three different places."

"Who the fuck is X?" John was livid. "What's X mean?"

"Xavier Blount. Not only that, but the bastard killed all your dad's stock, right down to the last goddam chicken and egg."

Agitated, John shook loose from Grace, walked to a nearby window and stared out in silence. *I should have come back sooner*, he thought to himself, and the blood began to pound in his temples.

Ty turned his chair toward John. "You know, your old man's heart ain't what it used to be. And Alan, well, nobody messes with Alan. He's fierce. He's a killer. X tried to recruit him, and Alan killed the man who made the offer." John stiffened. "But mention X and he turns white as a ghost."

64

John turned. Grace didn't recognize him. He scared her. "What's the status up there now?"

"They haven't had work in three months. The wolf ain't exactly at the door," Ty looked down. "You know, I'm not exactly your dad's favorite person, but I've tried to help him out." He looked back up at John. "He's let me, but you can tell it burns his ass something fierce."

"That all?" John was clinical.

"No. They shoot at his house at all hours, and last week they tried to burn the barn. They would have done it, too, except it was set poorly. Easy to put out."

John turned back to the window. "No way he'll buckle under," he whispered.

"Kids won't leave him either. He asked me to take 'em, I said okay, but they stick by him. They're good kids." Ty took another drink. "One more thing."

"Say it."

"Every time your dad refuses to grant X land, he demands another acre," Ty snorted. "Shit. Kinda like the opposite of compromise, or negotiations, but that's how this bastard works."

John breathed deep. "Well," he said to everyone, "I'm off." Grace went to his side as John bent to his uncle. "I'll be back for my friends ASAP."

Ty nodded. Grace was not pleased with this. "I'm going, too."

Grabbing her gently but firmly by the shoulders, he said with finality, "You're staying here until I can size things up. Understand?"

She nodded.

"I'm not exposing anyone here to danger." He looked at Ty. "You're safe with this man." John smiled at Ty, who smiled proudly back.

"It's good you're back, Johnny. Take my truck." He threw John the keys, and he was off.

5

The tiny Fox River Village just about split the distance between the town of Seney and the rocky shores of Lake Superior. John's drive was uneventful, but his mind was burning at the insult to his family, a thought that even took precedence over meeting his father again after six years with no contact or communication.

The half-hour drive whizzed by as scant minutes. The first thing to come into view was the partially-burned small barn, which indicated the south border of his father's 200 acres. The place looked rundown. John took this as a bad sign. If his family wasn't working, then what the hell *were* they doing? His dad always took pride in the way the place looked, but the weeds were taking over. The killing frost was overdue, but his dad still had crops in the fields. *Oh Christ,* John thought, *this is a bad scene.*

He wheeled his uncle's big and shiny Dodge Ram into the driveway. Borrowing his uncle's truck, a familiar vehicle, was an excellent idea. *Where's Rex?* he thought, and then shuddered. *Not the dog, too.*

Suddenly the big German Shepherd tore around the side of the farmhouse barking furiously. John breathed a sigh of relief as he jumped from the truck. "Rexy, goddamn!" he yelled at the big dog, who jumped and licked at John excitedly as he bent down to pet and hug his long-missed canine buddy. "How are you, boy!"

He glanced around Rex's head and saw his father standing about 50 yards away at the corner of the house, and his brother Alan running toward him at full speed. Both were armed. His dad, John was certain, toted his trusty Remington 870 shotgun, and the gun Alan had looked like a Mini-14, poor man versions of John's rifle. John stood to meet Alan's enthusiastic embrace.

John bearhugged his brother. Alan, always the emotional one, wept freely at seeing his brother, whom he worshipped as a boy and missed terribly. John noted over Alan's skinny shoulder that his father had not moved.

The two brothers pulled back to look at one another. Alan was still skinny, but hard as steel. He was 18 and just out of high school when John left to join the Olympic team in Korea. He had not seen him since. Though only 24 now, his hair had started thinning, but the steely blue eyes still shone with vitality and mischief. John noted with brotherly pride that, as overcome with emotion as Alan was, he would not put down his rifle, and every few seconds scanned the vista reflexively for signs of trouble.

They walked to their father (who had not moved an inch during the fraternal reunion), Rex barking in happy circles around the two men. John stopped at the edge of his father's aura. "Hi, Arthur," he said to his dad. "It's good to see you."

His father smiled warmly and reached over to embrace his prodigal son, who returned to him just when he needed him the most. He kept him in his embrace for quite a while, fighting back tears and avoiding the eyes of Alan. Arthur was not the emotive type, and though John had always scorned him for his stolid and austere disposition (no one, for example, would ever think of calling him "Art"), John realized that he was exactly the same way himself. At length, Arthur released his son.

"How did you find out?" he asked John.

"I didn't know. I was living down south near that chemical plant that was blown."

"Yeah. We heard about that."

"Anyway. It seemed like a visit was in order. I stopped by Ty's first to say hi. He told me."

"Ty's been good to us. Come on in," Arthur herded his boys toward the side door. "Your sister will be home soon," he shot John a not altogether benign look. "She hasn't seen you since she was ten, she'll probably die of shock."

"Twelve, Arthur," John corrected as he walked through the doorway. "Not ten, twelve. You still exaggerate."

"I never exaggerate," he pointed to the couch. "Sit down."

His father, characteristically, came right to the point in a long but succinct review of his encounter with Xavier Blount and his organization.

The breakdown of law and order in the rural areas had allowed X, a convict who had come from Wisconsin, to build an incredibly effective organization that was marked by rapacious and extreme violence against those who stood in his way, and he did it in three short years. Arthur then provided a profile of X.

Xavier Blount was a giant who often carried out his death sentences himself, and according to all who knew him, enjoyed this part of the job the most. X was extremely intelligent in a most clever, cunning, and guileful way. Physically, he was massive and intimidating and wore leather no matter what the climate. He surrounded himself with luxury and women, and orgies of totally outrageous character were the rule at The Palace, as his headquarters was known, which lay a few miles southwest of Grand Marais. His rule was absolute, and his influence, which by now extended across the whole eastern half of the Upper Peninsula, was pervasive and solid. The red helmets were no match for X and his establishment – they were spread too thinly and were too badly organized.

If X favored you, then your life would be relatively undisturbed, and you may even prosper. To be looked upon benignly by X, one had simply to do what one was asked. Usually that would be nothing at all. Some would be asked to part with livestock or produce. Some, like Arthur, to yield land for whatever purpose, often to grow marijuana, which X was free to cultivate without harassment. Many young men, eager for power and life in the fast lane, would aspire to become X-men. They would rise in a military-like hierarchy and receive rewards upon advancement. New trucks, a nice house (often taken from a dissenter), the best firearms, and other material goods of all descriptions could belong to those who did the bidding of their master in the all-important strongarm duties that were the essence of the organization.

But woe to any who refused X. They would be destroyed, suddenly or gradually, as it amused or suited the purposes of Xavier Blount.

And Arthur would not give in.

As preliminary punishment, he and his family had lost their employment, all three on the same day – Andrea at the dairy, Alan at the gunsmithy, and Arthur himself at Johnson's Orchards, where he worked part-time. The livestock thefts came next and were done at gunpoint. This, his father said, choked with angry tears, was the most embarrassing moment in his life. They had waited until Alan and Andrea were not at home and invaded the Wheelwright's farm. They were not rude, they were very business-like, but this was poor comfort to the completely dignified Arthur.

Last week, they tried to torch the barn.

"If X is so all-powerful, why doesn't he stamp you out like a bug?" John demanded.

"Two reasons," his father replied. "He wants the land *legally*. He's asked for 20 acres; now he's up to 25. He wants my name on the deed. Secondly, they're having a ball doing it like they're doing it."

"Johnny! O my god"

John turned and saw his little sister in the doorway. She ran and gave him a long hug. She was 18 now, a real woman, and he hardly recognized her. She was still skinny, but the days were gone forever when anyone would mistake her for a boy. His father smiled at this reunion and put a cap on the previous somber and urgent conversation. The three siblings chatted away while Arthur worked in the kitchen to pull together a little snack for them all. He returned with four beers while the hamburgers fried.

"Good beer," John observed after a long guzzle. "Ty made it, right?"

"Like I said," Arthur looked a little resigned. "Ty's been pretty good to us."

It occurred to John that his dad would have to be in dire straits to give up his John Adams. Maybe he didn't even have beer money. He stood up. "Alan," he called to his brother across the room. "Come here a second." They stepped back out into the yard.

"How's Arthur's heart?"

Alan shrugged. "I think it bothers him sometimes. All of a sudden, he'll just sit down wherever he is, or no matter what he's doing, takes deep breaths, looks kind of pale. Maybe it happens a little more these days, but no more than once a week, even now. Shit, you know Arthur – he never complains no matter what."

"Yeah, right. How's his finances?"

"Totally fucked." They both breathed a weak laugh.

"How bad?"

"He needs $4,000 or he'll lose the farm," Alan said flatly. "The farm is his, after that. Worked his balls off for 30 years on this place and might lose it now to foreclosure." He shook his head.

"Burgers!" the brothers heard Arthur call, and they went back inside.

After a most pleasant meal-time reunion and the attendant small-talk which broke John back into the fold, John called his dad outside.

"Here's $5,000," John handed his dad the huge wad of $100 bills.

"Where did you get it?" he asked without batting an eye.

There was a long, uncomfortable, but familiar pause that John tried to shake off. When he spoke, he tried to sound like a man, not like a boy making excuses to his father. "Listen to me, Arthur," he began calmly. "I worked hard for that money, and when I came out here, I knew it would come in handy. I just had a feeling. Now. There's $4,000 for the big debt, and the rest for living expenses until this X thing is settled. Along with a little more to buy some real beer." He was happy to end on a little joke.

"I'll take it, son," Arthur smiled and examined his oldest boy with a long look. "You know, this is the family's farm after I die. I can't let it go. Consider it a loan," he gave John a smile.

"One more thing," John said quietly. "I didn't come here alone."

Arthur was listening.

"I took a little black boy with me when I evacuated. I also have another fellow, named Chris, a good guy, who saved my ass on the way up here."

"Well," his father shrugged, "any friend of yours is a friend of mine."

"And I have a woman with me."

"That right?" Arthur smiled. "Well, where the hell is this entourage of yours?

It was decided that John would return to Ty's and bring the whole group back to the Wheelwright farm. Everybody, Ty and Jean, too.

When John returned from Ty's, Alan took him on a 'swamp cruise.' It had been six years since they lit up a joint together and drove the backroads of the big Seney swamp, which used to be a National Wildlife Refuge back when such a thing could exist. They ambled north on Driggs River Road and laughed about their boyhood. John told his brother about all that had transpired these last couple of days.

"Man, you've come a long way," Alan croaked to John, holding in a lungful of smoke and offering his brother the joint. "I can't believe you did all that stuff." He exhaled in a long blow while John took the joint from his fingers. "Man, you were always Mister Straight. You used to get really pissed off at me for the littlest things."

"Like blowing up police cars?" John smirked at Alan and took a long toke.

"There was just the one, and no one ever got hurt," Alan laughed. "You remember my 'Semtex stage'? Making explosives is good stuff to know these days. Besides, that ain't nothing compared to what you did, anyway."

"I guess not."

The brothers smoked for a few minutes in silence, enjoying the swamp sights and sounds as they plodded their way up the trail. This time of year, lovely warm days were precious and to be enjoyed. The sun would be down in another hour, and there was still not a cloud in the sky. The brothers were thoroughly stoned, and their thoughts ran wild.

"How come you never came home after you won the Silver Medal in Korea?" Alan asked.

John took a deep breath and considered his answer carefully. "I was ashamed."

"We were really proud of you, though." Alan shook his head. "What the hell were you ashamed of?"

"I told everybody I was going to win; I got beat by a little prick who wasn't as good as me," John paused. "And I needed to find my own way for a while. I couldn't stand the thought of going home to Arthur. We didn't get along very well back then, remember?"

Alan stared at his brother. "If the little prick wasn't as good as you, then how come he beat you?"

"Because he made me hate him." John suddenly had to laugh. "Alan, you wouldn't believe what a rude, smartass asshole this little English bastard was! Turns out he was just trying to get to me. I met him after the ceremony and he was completely different. He was gentle and polite, he didn't even have that cockney accent he was affecting. It was all an act! Man, I felt like a royal fucking jerk."

"Well, we missed you. Arthur pretended that he didn't – you know him – but he did, man." He paused to stare at a distant flock of geese. He looked at John. "You should've called, man. You were dead for all we knew."

John was getting annoyed by this line of questioning. "I had to do what I did, Alan. I can't be sorry for that and I ain't. But I'm back, and I'm glad I'm back."

The brothers noted how completely filthy Ty's shiny new truck had become since John got hold of it, and they vowed to wash it together tomorrow. They vowed all sorts of crazy nonsense when they were this stoned.

A few hours later, all were gathered about the big fireplace at the Wheelwright's home. The atmosphere was festive despite the recent unpleasantness concerning X and his enterprise. It was a true welcoming home of the prodigal son. Arthur pulled out all the stops this night, and everyone got along with everyone else so well that it was impossible to believe that a day ago most of them were strangers. Grace felt like a celebrity on John's arm. Jalen wrestled with Alan, who would make the amusing mistake of 'teaching Jalen chess' later in the evening. Ty and Arthur were going over old stories together with much loud laughter, and Chris had found someone to discuss poetry with in the attentive and refreshingly earthy Jean, who looked younger than she did a few hours ago. There was good food, excellent beer (homemade and otherwise), and the fine wine from Grace's cellar. Andrea was flitting about, playing the hostess, and getting to know the visitors. Fine Cuban cigar and pot smoke mingled in the cool evening air of the sitting room, and, as with the best parties, there was much friendly inebriation, but no one was smashed or obnoxious.

By the wee hours, only Arthur, Ty, and John remained active. Alan was snoring softly on a nearby chair, and the rest of the party had distributed themselves upstairs for some sleep. The three non sleepers had consumed the most alcohol but seemed the least affected. Arthur kept the fire at a nice, constant glow. It seemed by now that all the partying was a prelude to the present, inevitable, conversation.

"But he won't leave you alone. He can't. He has too much to lose if he compromises," Ty put forth.

"He's never compromised," Arthur said, and added promptly. "And neither do I."

John listened and said nothing.

"You know, Arthur," Ty said carefully, "you must know by now that you have two choices: give him the land, or..."

"Which I will never do."

"Or, confront him." Ty paused to let the phrase sink in. "If you don't, then I have a fear that you, and maybe the kids, too, will be dead in a week. I'd bet that it's not like X to drag a thing like this out. As soon as it stops being fun, he'll put an end to all this crap," he snapped his fingers, "just like that."

Arthur shot Ty a defiant look. "You think I should give in?"

"No. I don't," Ty answered. "But you need a plan."

A moment passed and John, with a voice of maturity and authority that surprised and pleased his father said, "X needs to be confronted. I'll meet with him."

Ty blew a soft raspberry and chuckled humorlessly. "So, you're gonna give X one more chance to change his ways, eh?"

John ignored this. "He'll want to meet. Umm..." he considered carefully and stroked his almost-beard. "Does anybody know X's habits?"

His father pointed to the sleeping Alan. "He might." John shook his brother awake and brought him up-to-date on the discussion.

"He goes to bars around here," Alan yawned, rubbed the sleep from his eyes, and became alert. "They party at The Palace most nights, but he goes to local bars sometimes. Not a lot."

"Let's meet him at one," John suggested. "As close to neutral a place as possible."

Alan was visibly upset at this proposition. "Shit, man, you don't know this guy. You *think* you do, but, man, he'll just *kill* you. Do you understand that?"

John looked back at his father. "Then we need to get a message to X." He turned again to Alan. "Do you know where any X-men hang out, so we can get a message to him through one of his people?"

"Hell, yes. Right down at Willy's. About five miles from here. It's a strip joint. Pretty wild. If we go there tomorrow night, we'll see ten of them son of a bitches there by closing time."

"Alright," John decided. "That's what we'll do. You comin' along?"

"Sounds like fun," Alan declared, glad that a direct confrontation with X, the only man he had ever feared, could be avoided.

"What are you going to say?" Arthur asked his eldest boy.

"I don't know," John replied and smiled at Ty, who was shaking his head. "I'll let you know tomorrow." He rose and stretched. "In the meantime," he yawned, "if anybody has any bright ideas, don't keep them to yourself."

"You gonna wash my goddam truck tomorrow?" Ty asked John in mock annoyance.

"Yeah, Ty. Sure."

Alan giggled from the couch.

John found the room upstairs containing his sleepy Grace and cozied in beside her, careful not to awaken her, and soon fell into a comfortable, dreamless, and much-needed sleep.

This was rudely interrupted an hour later by an explosion in the side yard. Like a bolt, Arthur and his two brothers were outside, followed by the others, all looking on the flaming remains of Chris' beautiful Buick.

6

There was no sleep, except for Jalen, at the Wheelwright farm that night. Chris was crestfallen at the total loss of his car, consoling himself as best he could that at least he had not left his computer in the blasted car. "Publish some of this stuff," he said bravely, "and buy a couple more cars."

John had less than $2,000 left of his original booty, and though he knew that everyone would pitch in, money would be tough coming until the present crisis was resolved. Until that time, John, Grace, Jalen, and Chris would stay at the farm. Ty and Jean (who had let the romantic devil Chris kiss her in the pantry last night because he had scratched out a little *haiku* for her) needed to get back to Ty's place. It was a market day, and Ty was itching for trade.

Arthur had lent a truck to a friend of his and offered this vehicle now to John, who would only have to pick it up to claim it as his own. It was decided, therefore, that Ty and Jean would drive John (and Grace for company) to pick up the truck, and then Jean would drive Ty back to his house. John welcomed this hour-long drive back to the farm, for he still didn't know how to handle the X situation, which he would have to begin to confront that evening.

While John and Grace were gone, Alan taught Chris how to use the old Mossberg pump gun. Chris was glad to help in a way that he was not accustomed to, firearms having never played a part in his life until now. Andrea, like all the Wheelwrights, was already an excellent shot and familiar with all standard weapon formats – something Arthur required of all his children as a part of their education. She had an AR-15 of which she was very possessive, and no one dared trifle with it without her permission, which was never given. They all stayed inside while John went to get his truck, but they kept a close watch on the farm.

"You know," Grace said softly to John as they waited for Ty and Jean to join them in the truck, "we haven't done it yet." She slid all the way against him to make room for the others and snuggled a bit.

Feigning bewilderment, John said, "Done what?"

"Never mind," Grace said curtly, straightening in the seat. John laughed and kissed her on the cheek.

The truck, a vintage model Ford 250 with a fiberglass cap, was a good one, John reckoned. The suspension was beefy enough for these backroads, and, except for a broken rear window on the cap, bald tires, a cracked windshield, no gas cap, rattles everywhere, and a conveniently broken odometer, all the essentials seemed to be in good repair. John was happy that the pickup had so much spunk, thanks to the big V-8. The brakes weren't the best, but that sorted well with John, who always felt that going was more important than stopping.

John and Grace were about 20 miles away from the farm now, bumping along the dirt road at a pretty fair clip. All the morning clouds and fog had vanished, and the autumn air had warmed considerably, a continuation of the unseasonably lovely weather they had been enjoying lately and would be sure to pay for later. *There is no time of year,* John thought, almost aloud, *that isn't completely awesome up here.*

Grace had been lulled asleep by the jostling truck, now resting gently against John's shoulder and breathing softly, while her hair would occasionally whip across his face, tickling his nose. He was about to nudge her over a bit to stretch his arm when he noticed a man bent over what appeared to be another fellow lying down in the road about 150 yards away. When the man saw John's truck he moved to the center of the road and waved wildly, signaling John to stop.

John nudged Grace awake. "What's going on?" she asked.

"I don't know. There's a guy down by the side of the road. Maybe he's hurt." John snuggled the .45 from his hip. "Steer for me, Grace," he ordered. He removed the magazine from the pistol and ejected the chambered round.

"What are you doing?" Grace wondered.

"Just a little precaution," he told her as he placed the ejected round into the magazine, slammed the magazine back into the gun, pulled the hammer back with his thumb, and put on the safety. He replaced the custom Colt on his hip underneath his sweater and reclaimed control of the truck.

The signaling man, a young, skinny, short fellow clad in very dirty overalls ran to the vehicle, now slowed to a stop a few yards from the downed man, who appeared to be unconscious.

"What's the problem?" John inquired from the truck.

"He's havin' a heart attack or somethin'!" the little man shouted at John, gesturing wildly in a come-and-see motion. "We was just walkin', and he grabs his chest and starts chokin' like. What do I *dooooo!*" the little man howled pathetically.

John and Grace climbed from the truck and ran toward the downed man, a very fat bearded fellow with an almost overpowering stench, who was now struggling to rise. The three of them helped the fat man to his feet. Gasping pathetically, he thanked the strangers breathlessly.

"Oh Lord," he gasped and grabbed John's arm. "Thank you. I think I'm alright." He stumbled, gasping for breath over to Grace and grabbed her arms. "Oh Lord, ma'am. Thank you. I think I'm okay, now."

With Grace still in his grip, he took a deep breath, stepped back a few feet, reached behind him and brought forth a huge Bowie knife which he held to the soft white neck of Grace, who knew better than to struggle. John glanced about him reflexively for the skinny man, who was behind him with a knife identical to the fat man's in one hand, and in the other, the keys to the pickup, which he ceremoniously dropped into his pants pocket.

Filled with anger at himself for being so easily duped, John thought of the .45 concealed on his hip but dared not go for it with Grace in the fat man's grasp.

"Now you listen to me if you wanna live!" Skinny yelled at John, with the big knife shaking in his dirty hand. "I'm gonna frisk you! And if you so much as make a funny move what I don't like, that bitch dies. And then you do too! You unnerstand?!"

"No need to shout." John looked over at Grace, who was securely locked in the fat man's grip but seemed calm.

"I'll fuckin' goddam shout, goddam it! Now put yer arms up in the air!"

John did as he was bid and felt directly the probing paws of Skinny rubbing over the pockets of his blue jeans. "I should be doin' this to the bitch," Skinny sniggered to Fatty, who replied: "I get to do it to the bitch. I won the flip."

John stiffened at the thought of the Human Pig touching Grace but kept his composure while Skinny relieved him of the spare contents of his pockets. Eventually, he nudged the .45.

"Holy shit! LOOK AT THIS!" he said as he struggled with the thumb release of John's holster, finally yanking the Colt free and holding it up to Fatty triumphantly.

"A gun!" Fatty cried in wonder.

"Not just a gun, this here's a *good* gun." Skinny glanced at John. "Ain't it, mister?" John was silent.

"Yep. This here's a genuwine Colt .45 pistol," Skinny swaggered as he walked a circle about John, pistol in one hand, blade in the other, his feeble mind reeling with his newfound importance in the universal scheme of things.

"We got a truck and a Colt .45." Skinny, clearly the brains of the outfit, stopped for a moment and considered his options. "Let's do the bitch," he said. He thought for a moment more, head up, hand on his chin, looking to John like a retarded person considering an algebra problem. "Then we'll kill 'em," Skinny decided finally.

Pig Man made a challenge to his boss's logic. "We don't need to kill them, really, do we?"

What's this? John wondered.

Skinny suddenly had a splendid idea. "Let's fuck the bitch and make him beg for mercy, and then maybe," he raised his eyebrows and grinned almost toothlessly at Fatty, "maybe, we'll let 'em both live!"

"If he begs good?" Fatty asked enthusiastically.

"Yeah, if he begs good!" Skinny and Pig Man laughed hysterically for a couple of seconds, then Skinny stopped abruptly, put his knife back in its sheath, and took the pistol in both hands. "Hmm," Skinny wondered aloud, examining the hardware. "Cocked and locked!" he exclaimed and looked at John. "You a cocked and locked cowboy, Mister Man-with-the-nice-bitch?"

Skinny put his thumb on the safety lever and snicked it off. "I know how to use this, fucker. Safety's off and I'll fuckin' blow your bitch away," he advised. "Unless you beg me."

Grace was then obliged to get down on her hands and knees. John could see the tension in her face, caught her eye, and gave her an almost comic wink. But for a few details, John knew what he was going to do, and wanted Grace at ease. Skinny grabbed her long locks with one hand, twisting the hair into a fist, securely leashing her head. With the other hand, he held the pistol to her head. John was about 15 yards from Grace.

"You first," he said to Fatty. "You get to fuck her first. And YOU, Mister Cocked-and-locked-cowboy mother-fucker," he yelled to John, "You take one step and I'll fucking blow her goddam head off!"

Skinny gave instructions. "Pull her pants down, but keep the knife ready," he ordered the Pig Man, who reached down and worked Grace's jeans down to her knees. "Spread them legs to get them pants all the way down!" Skinny commanded. Grace felt her knees forced apart against the hard gravel, and a twinge of pain crossed her face. John's muscles tensed like a tiger. Fatty was exploring Grace's soft bottom through little red panties, but she knelt perfectly still and made not a sound.

"You start beggin' now, asshole!" the skinny one yelled to John, "or I'll kill her after we fuck her." Fatty looked up at his boss.

"I ain't killing nobody," Fatty said defiantly.

With that fatal remark, John relaxed, for he knew that the Human Pig would have no part of killing.

"*I'll* kill 'er then!" he turned and yelled to John, giving him a wild-eyed look. "Okay, now let's see that ass." Skinny was not screaming now, but intent on the work at hand. The fat thug cuffed two filthy thumbs in the waistband of Grace's underpants and began a slow slide down the sides of her thighs. Skinny craned his neck for a better look, as John knew he would.

At that moment John began his careful rush upon Skinny, who turned instantly and noiselessly to John, leveled the pistol and pulled the trigger, which simply clicked as the hammer fell on the empty chamber that John had prepared. John easily snatched the stunned Skinny's wrist with his left hand and punched him on the side of the face with his right fist, knocking him to his knees. John twisted the gun from the thug's hand, racked the slide of the big pistol and expertly double-tapped two hollowpoints through his chest – thus was Skinny's instant demise. *Now Pig Man,* thought John calmly, and he turned upon him.

Though the situation appeared to be most serious, John's overwhelming thought was the stupidity of these sorry highwaymen.

"Jesus Christ, what morons," he whispered as he faced the fat thug, who had backed off and stood now about 30 feet from John, with his big bowie tucked under the chin of Grace, who hung silent and perfectly still in the robber's grasp, eyes expressionless, blue jeans and panties framing her knees.

John had a two-handed hold on the .45, a few inches low of aiming position. "Let her go and I'll let you live," John hollered to the fat man, who was extremely agitated.

"Fuck you," the thug yelled back, now slowly moving backward with Grace tightly pulled against him. Only the Pig's eyes and forehead, and the thick black knit cap which crowned him, were visible above Grace's own head. "You throw me your gun and I'll let her go." John kept pace with the thug's backward pace.

"And don't come closer to me!" the thug yelled, still backing up. John stopped, knew that the fat thug would soon be out of range and noticed a thin line of blood running down Grace's white neck. John reflexively raised the Colt to aim and fired without hesitation.

Fatty spun around and fell face-first into the grass. Grace frantically restored her clothing while running as fast as she could into the arms of the much-relieved John, who noticed that the thin line of blood was nothing more than a slender thread of black yarn which had pulled free from her collar.

"I wasn't afraid," Grace whispered into John's neck as they stood together in a grateful embrace. He could feel her heart pounding. "You sure are a good shot," she said.

"It wasn't as hard as all that. It was a pretty easy shot, actually. I wouldn't have taken any chances with you. We were lucky that those morons were so, well," he fished around for the right word, "moronic." They laughed, flushed with relief, and John kissed Grace's forehead. "Stay here while I take a look at that guy."

A strange mix of short-term relief and budding new anxiety washed over John as he walked over to pick up the knife which had spun free from the thug's grasp. He squatted down to examine it. It was a poorly-made bowie pattern with a plastic handle to which a stainless blade, marked MADE IN HONDURAS, was imperfectly attached. John ran his thumb across the blade. *Sharp, anyway,* he thought to himself. He stood and tossed the knife into the tall summer weeds of the roadside.

A few yards away lay the fat thug, who was not yet dead, but was well on his way to the happy robbing grounds. The bullet had entered above his right eye and exited above the right ear. The fat thug was unconscious and panting a-rhythmically, with one bloodshot eye completely open. John wondered if he should administer the *coup de grace,* something he would have done even for a run-over skunk, but then remembered the thug's filthy hands fondling the sweet little butt of the woman he was growing to love, and thus he declined to relieve the thief of any further suffering which nature may yet have in store for him.

John checked the fat man's pockets and found $70. *Now I am a killer and a corpse-robber, too,* he thought as he put the seven $10 bills into his jeans' pocket. He looked over his shoulder – Grace was facing the sun, away from him, while John had robbed the body. He felt grim but strangely curious as he glanced over to the skinny thug, whose corpse was doubled over near a big maple tree. This time Grace was looking at him. *What does it matter, anyway,* he thought, striding over to the body, squatting down, and patting the pockets of the dead man. He made a show of his macabre doings.

"Keys," he shouted, pocketing the chain and jingling keys recovered from the pants pocket of the corpse, beginning the grisly inventory. Grace looked away. John continued. "Wallet," he shouted next.

"John," Grace interrupted. "It's okay."

Embarrassed but relieved, he searched the wallet and found nothing of interest. About to abandon the body, John gave the shirt pocket a cursory pat and felt a soft bulge, reached inside, and pulled out yet another wad of money and examined it. "Another $70," he turned and said to Grace, who gave a noncommittal smile and looked away. "They must have taken $140 from some poor son of a bitch and split it up," he observed.

John strode back to Grace, who was now sitting on a big rock near the road, face tilted up to the sun, eyes closed. *God, what a beauty,* John thought as he reached out to stroke her soft dark hair. Grace turned and opened her eyes and awarded John a sweet smile as she took his hand and kissed it. John's brow darkened with a long-dreaded thought. *My match ammo is gone now,* he thought gloomily of the two magazines-full of the old Remington ammo he had left in his rig. *Now my gun is just a gun.*

"Let's get out of here, Grace," John said as he helped the slender girl to her feet. "Let's go back to the farm." At that, they climbed into the truck and left the scene of John's double-handiwork.

Back at the Wheelwright's, Alan identified the pair of highwaymen from John's description. "A couple of retards from Marquette," is how he described them, sitting with Grace and John on the back porch, tearing into a recently deceased chicken. "Wanna piece?" he offered Grace, who took a piece of white meat. "They've been waylaying folks for the last couple of weeks around here. Travelers, mostly. Probably living in the woods. They didn't recognize you, so they went for you."

"Well," John smiled at his brother, "They're dead now." Grace shuddered at this conversation as the sight of her own husband lying dead in the grass with three bullets in his chest flashed through her mind.

"Good job, brother." Alan held up his beer in salute, and then looked deep into John's eyes and spoke softly. "Interesting feeling. Isn't it?"

John let it go by. "One thing, Al," he said to his brother as he glanced toward the open porch door.

"I know, I know. You don't want anybody else to know about this until this X thing is over. Right?"

"Thanks."

"Good idea, actually." Alan gestured toward the house. "Who needs more problems?"

After a hurried dinner of more chicken and another beer each, the brothers decided to get the X-man business over with as soon as possible. John had kept his thoughts regarding the evening encounter with the X-men pretty much to himself and assured his father that he had everything under control. John and Alan headed for the bar.

The recently-acquired truck hobbled down a particularly poor patch of road on the way to Willy's, squeaking badly in the left front area.

"Goddamn it," John was annoyed. "Every ten minutes I find something else fucked up about this goddam truck."

Alan tried, and failed, to stifle his laughter, which brought a threatening look from John. "Just relax, man," Alan advised his brother. "It was still a good deal."

"Sonofabitchin' gas gauge hasn't gotten off of 'full' since I got it."

The brothers passed a tacky billboard on the roadside assuring thirsty pilgrims that their quest would soon be rewarded.

YOU'RE ON THE ROAD TO WILLY'S
– 3 MILES –
LIQUOR - LIVE MUSIC - LIVE GIRLS

"Pretty classy!" John opined. "Apparently the girls are actually alive." The brothers laughed and talked about nothing in particular, enjoying the night in spite of the serious business ahead of them.

Back home Andrea was teaching Grace how to shoot the extra Mini-14 from the Wheelwright arsenal. Jalen had been taken to Ty's place to be tended by Jean.

Ty stayed at the Wheelwright farm where he hoped he would not be needed, but no one doubted that he would be a handy fellow to have around if his services were required. Ty wasn't much for "mouse-guns," as he called them, and constantly twitted Andrea in a good-natured way about her .223, which always made her irate and indignant. Ty favored his proven Remington 300 Magnum with a Redfield 4-12X scope. This was a better long-range gun than anything Arthur had in stock – the custom 7mm Magnum in a Sako action and McMillan stock laying against the fireplace was the closest Arthur could come. If things got close in and hairy, the Ruger Redhawk in .44 Magnum strapped to the side of Ty's wheelchair in a custom-made holster would prove a solace.

It was another clear, warm, humid night in a memorable series for John, who wheeled the big Ford into the driveway of Willy's and parked in the rapidly filling lot. It was about 9 pm, opening time for the famously sleazy Willy's.

"You know," Alan said to John as he shut the truck off, "it ain't fair for you to keep your plans to yourself."

His brother paused a moment and gave Alan a friendly look. "Brother, I'm not keeping anything from you. I don't know what to do, really. If things are like you say, then I won't be able to get within 100 yards of X without being shot." He looked at Alan for confirmation.

"Ah!" Alan said. "It's finally starting to sink in!"

"And so, I don't know what to tell these guys to go back and tell X." They sat in thoughtful silence for a minute. "I thought about it all day."

"Me too," Alan allowed.

"Let's go in and have a drink." And so, they locked the new truck (which John discovered would not lock on the passenger side), and after some colorful condemnation of the door lock, John led the way into Willy's.

Monday was No Music Nite, live bands being the secondary attraction here at Willy's, and John was most grateful for the coincidence. The pair found a booth near the door after two meaty bouncer-types approved of their existence and allowed them in to partake of the wonderland that was Willy's.

The decor was typical up-north rustic. The room was about 30 feet wide and 120 feet long, with booths and Formica-topped tables running most of the way, leaving space for two pool tables and a dartboard at the other end of the room. The bar itself was made of nice, thick wood, and took up the middle half of one long wall. Two small stages flanked the bar, and there was a jukebox blazing country rock next to the stage at the far end. Behind the bar was the inevitable W I L L Y 'S in red and green neon lights blazoned across the wall. It buzzed annoyingly. The floor was cheap tile, but the ceiling was stamped tin, quite elaborate, and lent a small touch of class to the otherwise totally deprived room, which wanted paint and was illuminated by a depressing yellow light that did nothing to flatter the naked and near-naked bodies of the young and not-so-young ladies waiting tables and about to do their routines. The unfortunate lighting was not a focus of contention among the regular patrons, who were happy enough just to see naked women, period. None of the talent, the brothers noted, was yet on display.

John hated places like this. Alan was indifferent. The joint was less than half full and strangely quiet, as though someone had died, and people were doing their best not to have too much fun. The door opened, and the bouncers let a party of three men and women through, obviously regulars with a good start on the night. They went back to the tables to "shoot some stick" as one of them suggested.

A pretty waitress who looked like Ojibwa tribe, Alan reckoned, came from behind the bar and asked the brothers what they required. She wore black bikini bottoms, soft-soled black boots, and no top. The brothers could not but admire her perky breasts, even in the drab yellow light. Two bottles of Molson were ordered, and the waitress asked if they wanted to run a tab. They said they would.

The door opened again, the bouncers permitting entrance of a young man whom Alan recognized immediately. "Bryan!" Alan hailed the lanky fellow, who returned the greeting and joined the brothers at the booth, sitting next to Alan.

Bryan was a former colleague of Alan's until Alan lost his job at the gunsmithy. They were the two senior apprentices. With Alan gone, the workload on Bryan was doubled, but so was his status at the shop. He ordered a double bourbon, straight up, water on the side. He was already half in-the-bag.

"Nice titties, eh?" Bryan critiqued as the waitress left the table. He bolted the liquor. John wished he would go away. "Listen, Alan," Bryan was suddenly maudlin. "Mike had to fire you, man. He didn't have no choice."

"I don't have any quarrel with Mike, Bryan."

"They came right in," Bryan whispered loudly. "I was in the back, and I heard 'em tell Mike that they'd torch the place." He gulped water and coughed. "You know them motherfuckers!"

"I've got no problem with Mike, okay?"

Bryan raised his head high and scanned the room, a confused look on his face. "What the hell s'matter with this place tonight?" He suddenly yelled out, "Zis a goddam funeral parlor or what! Waitress!" he giggled and fell back into his seat. John stiffened a bit and wondered if he should show this fellow the door. He remembered the business at hand and, thinking better of it, decided to suffer this fool in silence until he moved on.

The waitress arrived with another round. "Willy says you got to calm down or else no more drinks," she said to

Bryan, who looked indignant. Bryan stared at the wall blearily. "Motherfuckin' X-men sons a bitches," he mumbled to the dirty panel. He tried to focus his stare on Alan. "If I was Mike, no way I'd give in to those X-men sons a bitches. I'd say, 'Fuck you, get outta my shop.' Goddamn it."

John tried to curb the monologue. He asked Alan, "What does X stand for again?"

"Xylophone," Bryan blurted and sniggered.

"Xenon," Alan offered.

"Xenon?" John asked.

"It's a gas, I think," Alan laughed.

"Xerox," from the giggling Bryan.

"X-ray," from Alan.

"Xantippe," John offered with a chuckle.

"What the fuck is a Zantibby?" Bryan slurred cheerfully.

"Socrates' wife," John explained.

"Oh yeah," Bryan belched. "I forgot."

The booth behind the giddy trio emptied slowly of three large men, biker-looking fellows. They surrounded John's booth. Many patrons of the bar made their exit at this point. After a moment, the booth creaked and rocked, and a pair of leather-clad legs swung huge boots to the floor. This man stood.

"X," boomed his deep voice, "stands for Xavier."

Except for a very nervous Willy, the bar emptied absolutely. John noticed a look of white fear on his brother's face, struggling for calm. Bryan began to whimper like a baby.

"Glad to meetcha," John said in a steady voice to the leather-clad giant standing next to him, who looked amused at John's effrontery. X grabbed John with both hands, lifted him out of the booth as if he were a sack of potatoes, lifted him high above his head, and slammed him in sitting position onto a nearby chair. John wisely hung loose as a doll and did not resist.

"Watch him," X ordered his three men, who unholstered pistols and leveled them at John's chest as he sat. They all had identical Glocks.

A smile curled the lip of X. "Willy!" he thundered. "Bring me a bottle of 151." Willy was happy to comply and did so without delay.

This rum was the favorite drink of X's, but only in public, his private tastes were much more refined. He poured himself about three fingers in a small tumbler and wedged his bulk down into John's vacated seat, facing the trembling pair.

X looked up at the ceiling, his face taking on an expression of pained toleration as if communing with some stern divinity. He looked back down and leveled a steady gaze at Bryan. "You know," X reached inside his jacket and retrieved a cigar, the end of which he bit off and spat to the floor, "my mother told me when I was a little boy, that people might make fun of my name because it was so unusual. And they did," X nodded. "They did." X rested the cigar between his teeth and continued slowly. "I was named after my grandfather. He was a free-spirited sort of man who was killed by a pack of cowardly lawmen right in front of my mother and my brothers." X took the cigar from his teeth. "I wasn't born yet. But mama was right," X grinned maliciously, "people have always made fun of the sacred name that my mama gave me."

X drained the glass of rum and put the cigar back between his lips. He sat staring at Bryan, who was breathing heavily, white as a ghost. After a few moments X raised a great gloved hand and pointed at the end of his cigar. Bryan frantically looked about the table for a match or lighter and grabbed the well-worn Zippo which Alan offered him.

With shaking hands Bryan leaned toward X's cigar. X raised himself up, seized Bryan's wrist, and guided the lighter toward the cigar. When the flame licked the tip, X let the cigar drop from his lips, grabbed the back of Bryan's head with his other hand, and sprayed the rum from his filled cheeks across the lighter flame. The effect was like a miniature flame-thrower blasting the screaming face of Bryan, locked inches away into X's iron grip.

"MY EYES! MY EYES!" Bryan shrieked into the laughing face of X, who lifted the thrashing man from his seat, and hurled him to crash *upside-down* against the wall, mercifully rendering the man unconscious, and concluding an act of savagery that John and Alan could not even have imagined. The three men guarding John never once took their eyes off him.

Next, X turned his attention to John. He pointed at Alan. "Guard him." The three men moved as one, turning to Alan's booth and leveling the pistols at his chest in unbroken concentration.

Pulling a chair up and turning it backward, X sat very close to John. He breathed a deep sigh and smiled peacefully. "Ahhhh," he looked into John's expressionless eyes. "The night is young, Mr. John Wheelwright."

He leaned forward, even closer to John. "John Wheelwright who robbed the Jew," he paused for effect. "John Wheelwright who beat the cop," he noted that John's eyes betrayed nothing. "John Wheelwright who bribed the bridge man." X rose majestically and walked slowly around John's chair. John noticed that X was much older than he had expected, around 50, he guessed. John reckoned him to be almost seven feet tall, maybe 350 pounds, but no fat. He had a nose like a hawk, and brown raptor eyes set deep into the skull that were at once piercing and oddly vacant. His thick black hair was pulled back into a pony-tail, held together with a silver clasp. He was immensely muscular.

"You stupid puppy," X stopped and laughed at John. "Why do you think that the bridge cop let you go? Because you said you weren't affiliated with my famous organization? Stupid puppy." X resumed his seat. "With all that extra money heading into my territory in such a panic, you were let through because that bridge cop thought you were one of my very own. Is this not ironic?"

John said nothing and tried to breathe regularly while making of his face an expressionless mask. He was never closer to death than at this moment, and he knew it.

X stood. "I want 30 acres of your father's land."

"I thought it was 25?" John snapped.

"Shhhhhhhhhhhhhhhhhhhhhhhhhhhh." X held a finger to John's lips. John looked away and listened. "Shut your stupid puppy jaws and listen to me. It's 30 now. I want it nice and legal, and I want it tomorrow. I will be by your house at noon with my lawyer and a few of my staff. I want your whole family there. If anyone leaves your property during the night, or before I arrive tomorrow, they're dead. Do you understand so far?"

John stared ahead and nodded affirmatively.

"Everyone outside, and *no weapons*. Do you understand *that*?"

Another nod.

"Good. If you try to interrupt or upset these plans in any way, then I will have a little gift for your sister Andrea." At this X clenched his groin with a massive gloved hand and smiled broadly. "And another little gift for your daddy."

In a blur X ripped a huge pistol from his jacket, turned on his heel and fired five monstrous blasts into the far wall of the barroom. John palmed both ears, but the first shot got through, almost deafening him.

"Willy! Bring that dartboard and show it to my puppy, here." X boomed, and Willy scrambled to comply. In seconds the anxious barkeep was at John's chair holding the dartboard to him as if it were a mirror. There was a single, large, ragged hole where the small wire circle in the middle of the board used to be. X holstered his gun, which John identified as a Desert Eagle in caliber .50. In his hand, it almost looked small.

"Daddy gets that, after watching his daughter get this," X repeated the clutching gesture at his groin.

X smiled a happy smile. "I might even eat the little nigger when I'm finished!" At this burst of high humor, even the bodyguards laughed heartily. He stared down on John and smiled like a benevolent father.

"Good night, puppy dog. You go now."

John rose from his chair. With a nod from their master, the guards backed off Alan, and the two brothers headed toward the door, glancing on the way at the still motionless body of the hapless Bryan. On the way to the truck, they noticed six topless, bikini-clad women with their arms crossed in front of them for warmth, who never even stopped to grab a shirt in their haste to evacuate. They were almost as glad to see John and Alan leave the bar as the brothers were to be leaving.

On the drive home, John and Alan noted the presence of sentries near the farm, and they had no doubt that X would make good on his threat to kill anyone who tried to leave.

"I wonder if Bryan's okay," Alan said quietly. "Man, he never even came to. And my ears are still ringing." He, like John, was filled with anxiety but happy to be alive at the same time. John did not answer this rhetorical question, and the pair rode home in silence. It was now about 10:15, and it was going to be another long and sleepless night.

When the brothers arrived at the farm, they sat with their father and uncle and told them all that had transpired that evening. A look of pain and resignation that no one had seen on Arthur's face since his wife's death seemed to drain from him all spirit of resistance. They sat in silence for long minutes. Suddenly, his father sprang to his feet.

"That's it. They got me," he paced. "I'm finished." He stopped and looked at Ty and his sons.

"It's even worse than that, actually," John noted calmly. "You see, there's no reason for X to keep you, or any of us, alive after you deed him the land. You're a trouble-maker, as far as he's concerned. I've watched this guy work," he smiled crookedly, "and your stock is gonna fall after this deal is done, even if it goes through with no one getting hurt."

More silence followed, the men sitting and racking their brains to see a hole in the scheme that X had laid forth. Finally, his father spoke in tense resignation. "Let's get some rest," he stood. "We can't be draggin' our asses tomorrow."

All agreed that it seemed pointless to stare at the walls all night, and they retired for what sleep they would be granted after agreeing on a schedule for guard duty during the night. A single sentry would be posted, the other three men agreeing to change watch every two hours.

But there was no rest to be had. Arthur had no intention of sleeping, he simply wanted the others to go away so he could meditate on the situation in whatever peace he could find.

He thought of his wife, Abby. He tried to imagine what advice she might give him if he could hear her soft voice once again. He recalled the births of his three children as if they were yesterday. They were all born at home, right here on the farm he was going to lose.

Arthur remembered, sitting in the dark, the day he taught John how to hold a pistol. He remembered the Ruger .22 Mark IV that he had given him for his tenth birthday, and how quickly he became an expert shot. His mind turned to his second-born, so different from John, and so much harder to control. Alan was always in trouble, but he was not a bad boy – he just attracted trouble like a magnet.

The farm was almost his. He had mailed the last payment, and soon his lawyer would bring him the deed that he had struggled 30 years to pay off. He recalled how he and Abby fell in love with the place at first sight, and how she made the house sing. All the little bits of love everywhere. Then he lost her. Then he lost John. Tears welled up in his eyes, and he blinked them back. *There was no use indulging this.* After all, John came back. Just in the nick of time, his oldest boy returned to him to help him see this through. He got on his knees and prayed to Jesus. He hated to ask anything from anyone, even from his God, but there was nothing else he could do now.

7

By dawn, Arthur had prepared a light breakfast for everyone. They all felt like prisoners. Arthur considered his sons and Ty (and Chris, though he did not know him very well) to be men struggling together, and with their own free wills, committed to seeing out the crisis. He did not feel this way about his daughter. Under house arrest, Arthur could not send Andrea out of harm's way, and this bothered him more than anything. He considered hiding her somewhere on the property but thought that might prove to be too antagonistic. She sensed this and tried to assure him that even if she could leave, she would not. Grace, of whom Arthur was becoming very fond, felt the same way, maintaining flatly that she would not leave John's side under any circumstances. They were an admirable crew. But everywhere and everyway Arthur considered this situation, he ran into the impenetrable wall.

They thought about using Chris as a sniper, but dismissed this on the grounds that X most likely knew about Chris's presence among them, and that Chris was hardly a sniper, anyway. There was no use calling out for help with the PC on the web or the cell, or satellite phone because there was no one to call. So, they sat and waited, and watched the clock.

In this time of waiting, Jalen was playing chess with himself at a little table in front of the house, a little too near the road for John's comfort. He was about to stroll down to tell Jalen to move back when a new Prius drove by, slowed down, turned around, and whizzed back to the house, pulling into the drive. Everyone was instantly on guard, but with no display of weapons.

A trim, well-dressed man got out, smiled, and addressed Jalen. "Hey, young man. I see you're having a game with yourself."

"Nobody will play me," Jalen moaned. Then he brightened. "Wanna play?!"

Addressing the family, now, the man said, "Does anyone mind if I have a game with the young fellow? I haven't played in years, and he looks like he can use some cheering up."

No one objected, but all were wary. The family got comfortable while the man took a chair opposite Jalen. The man gave Jalen white and the first move. Jalen gleefully rubbed his little hands together, then took out his pawn.

It took about 20-minutes before Jalen yelled a 'bad word' and pushed the table over, running, crying hysterically, into the house.

"What the hell?" John said, and Arthur, John, and Alan all ran down to the road. The man stood with his hands in the air in a gesture of surrender.

John asked, "What just happened?"

The man replied, "He lost. I guess it doesn't happen very often. He's an amazingly gifted child."

"I never saw it happen ever," John said, adding derisively, "So you couldn't let the child win the game?"

The man was honestly surprised at John's objection. "He's no 'child' at a chessboard; he's a… a *shark* with *rabies!*" The man dropped his hands and smiled sadly. "I haven't had a game like that in ages."

"Who are you?"

"They call me Skinner. I'm Xavier Blount's legal counsel."

Alan spoke. "Mister, you got balls like cantaloupes or else you're one dumb son of a bitch to be here right now."

Skinner was as calm as a corpse. "Little of both, probably."

Arthur walked up to Skinner, almost nose-to-nose. "State your business."

"Nobody knows I'm here," Skinner said.

"Yeah. Right," Alan sneered. Arthur gave him a look that would keep him quiet for the duration.

He turned back to Skinner. "I asked what was your business."

"You need to leave. Just go. Now. You're out of time. There's no way this ends with any of you alive."

"That's not going to happen," Arthur said. "And what do you care?"

Skinner dropped his head and closed his eyes, rubbing his forehead like he had a headache. "You know," he said, "I don't agree with a lot of things that X does. But this. This is… a stupid tragedy. About to happen." He looked up at the three men, then at the rest of the family behind them, and sensed the futility of his request.

"Okay," he concluded. "I had to say something. I had to stop by. And try. At least."

Skinner gave a little wave and turned to get back to his car, opened the door, and retrieved two books from the back seat. He straightened and said, "Good luck, all. And tell Jalen he's the second-best chess player in the entire U.P." He tossed the two books gently onto the grass. "These are for him. If he lives through this. If X doesn't eat him." He waved again, resumed the driver seat, and sped away.

About 11:30, they went back out to the front yard, sitting and pacing about the porch. Chris stayed inside with Jalen, out of harm's way. Or that was the hope. The beautiful weather of the past few days seemed about to turn.

John felt strange being unarmed, without even his trusty Ek No.5, an original, to keep him company with its unique brand of cold steel reassurance.

X and his entourage were right on time.

They came in three new cars, two ancient red Lincoln Town Cars, with a black Cadillac Escalade sandwiched between them in stately procession. They pulled into the drive and insolently turned to array themselves across the front lawn about twenty yards from the porch. Out of the backseats of each Town Car spilled three armed men. Two from each car toted AK-47s, and the remaining men had identical custom bolt-action rifles, heavy guns with thick barrels, and scopes. These men were sharpshooters. They all spread themselves out in a semi-circle about the front yard, with the snipers on each flank. X was evidently big on the overkill sort of mentality.

The front passenger of the big cars was next to exit after the riflemen were in place, but the drivers stayed with their vehicles. These two men went over to the Escalade and opened the doors. X exited from the driver's side, pausing to hold open the seat to permit an elderly gentleman in a three-piece suit to struggle out of the back seat with his briefcase.

From the passenger side emerged an exotically beautiful woman, wrapped in fur. She looked like a countess, late twenties maybe, thought John. She waited for X to come around to her, and she took his arm. The pair approached the porch.

"I see everyone is here," X smiled. With a nod from their master, the two door-openers became friskers of the besieged Wheelwrights and their friends. This was done quickly and professionally. When they were finished, they fell back each to one side and a little behind X and his lady-friend.

"Our greetings to the Wheelwrights and friends," X said with an exaggerated elegance. He indicated the woman on his arm. "This is Tanya." He stroked her cheek, and she smiled up at him. "She is a special woman." He indicated the gentleman behind him, whom he ushered forward into view of the others. "This is my attorney, Mr. Kenneth LaPlace. Tanya, Ken, meet Mr. Arthur Wheelwright."

As if reaching into a toilet bowl to squeeze a turd, Arthur took the hand of the lawyer and shook it briefly. He nodded courteously to Tanya, who offered her hand to Arthur, who let it hang there.

"Where Tanya is from, Mr. Wheelwright," X instructed with a hint of impatience, "a kiss of the hand is considered an appropriate and courteous gesture." Arthur complied perfunctorily and stepped back.

"I have promised Tanya that she should be especially amused today," X said, eyeing his mistress lustily. "You see, it's her birthday. You would do well to anticipate every courtesy to her."

X motioned to the lawyer, who opened his briefcase and removed a few papers. X turned to Arthur. "Mr. LaPlace has drawn up a contract between you and me. I presume you have the necessary papers handy?" Arthur nodded. "Excellent. Please take a moment now to read these." He nodded to his lawyer, who passed the papers to Arthur, and relieved Arthur of his little sheaf in exchange.

Tanya sighed and pouted ever so slightly. X consoled her. "It is a dry procedure, my dear. It will take but a moment." Arthur read the papers as Tanya surveyed the Wheelwrights and their friends. She brightened suddenly and beckoned X to bend to her. He stooped low, and she whispered into his ear. X smiled. "Perhaps you're right, my dear," he said, straightening.

"Will the two ladies please come forward?" X commanded. The men became very apprehensive. What would happen, they wondered, and how much could they endure? X looked at Arthur, who stared right back at the monster who tormented him. "Mr. Wheelwright, you've nothing to fear. Please continue your perusal of the documents at hand."

The two women made their way forward and stood in front of X and Tanya. "May I introduce Grace, I believe, and Andrea," X was gallant. Tanya held out her hand, which each woman took and kissed. Tanya looked them over carefully, walking now behind the two women. She stopped and stroked Andrea's back gently. "She looks like a boy from behind," she called to X in an accent that John could not recognize.

Nodding agreement, X laughed softly. "Andrea is skinny but not without her attractive qualities," X called back. Though Arthur pretended to read the documents, his attention was riveted on the plight of the women.

Tanya came back to view Andrea from the front. "You are right," she said and softly stroked Andrea's breasts through her fuzzy sweater. Andrea breathed deeply and sighed. "Oh my!" Tanya chirped. "Are you excited, or afraid?" Tanya turned to X, who joined her in cordial laughter.

X's woman moved to Grace. "But this one, my darling Xavier," she crooned, smitten with Grace's beauty, "this one is very nice." She gently caressed Grace's breasts. "Turn around," Tanya commanded softly. Grace complied and closed her eyes to avoid looking at her friends. Tanya pulled the tucked-in shirt free from Grace's jeans and tugged the shirt up gently. "Goodness, Xavier, look at this

skin. It is radiant!" she called as she massaged the nakedness above her beltline. She leaned down and kissed her at
the curve of her hip.

"I am delighted at your pleasure, my dear," X assured
his beautiful and lascivious consort. X dismissed the
women, who promptly returned to their positions near the
porch. Andrea, John noticed, was crying. He tensed. What
next?

"Mr. Wheelwright!" X boomed, his mood turning
suddenly businesslike. "I presume you are ready to complete our transaction."

Arthur nodded.

"Good. Come forward."

Slowly, but with no pretense at dignity or defiance,
Arthur walked up and stood before X, who towered almost
a full foot above him. X slapped him hard.

The brothers moved a step, but Arthur stopped them
with a gesture. The men with the rifles were very attentive.
"That," X thundered, "was for making this procedure un-
necessarily complex, and wasting so much of my time over
these few weeks!" Tanya, tremendously excited, reached
out and touched X with a trembling hand. Arthur stood
impassive.

"Now," he gestured to the lawyer and turned back to
Arthur. "Here is a pen. Sign these papers."

Arthur took the pen and a clipboard from the lawyer. A
drop of blood fell from Arthur's nose onto the contract.
Tanya moaned. "Oh. No!" she called to Arthur, interrupting his gesture. "Don't wipe your nose. Let the blood run."

Wow, John thought to himself. *This is one twisted bitch.*

X smiled and kissed Tanya's cheek. "My dear, sometimes you surprise even me." He turned back to Arthur.
"Sign," X said with a note of terrible finality. Arthur let the

blood stream down his lip, over his chin and on to his shirt. He put the pen to paper.

"Wait," X looked inspired. Arthur paused and looked into the dark eyes of his oppressor. "Get on your knees."

"What?"

"I said," he kissed the other cheek of his mistress and smiled at her. "I said to get on your knees to sign the papers."

John snapped. "No!" he yelled from the porch. Arthur turned to quiet his son, but he did not descend to his knees. X's brow darkened, and he looked pained. John and Alan recognized this look as the one that preceded the assault on the unfortunate Bryan the evening before. Tanya squeezed X's arm, squirming with anticipation, and obviously enjoying her birthday. X sure knew how to show a girl a good time.

"My stupid puppy demands special treatment," X said to all. "Come down here!" he thundered at John, who made his way to the black-clad giant in a few quick strides, stopped in front of him, *and smacked X across his granite face* in a gesture that was plainly meant to insult.

The four gunmen with the AKs ran forward and thrust the barrels of their weapons at John. X's eyes bulged slightly, and he looked with amazement at the defiant John.

"I challenge you to a duel, you coward bastard," John, trembling with anger, yelled up at X, who recovered quickly from the brief shock of the slap. Nothing like this had ever happened before. X wondered how to kill John in the most spectacular manner manageable – there were so many ways at hand. In a flash, he decided to strangle him on the spot, but was interrupted by Tanya, who hugged X before he could raise his arms.

"A duel!" she panted. "This is the most wonderful birthday," and she squeezed him tightly. X stared down at John and began laughing.

John continued his challenge. "Pistols. If you win you get the farm and everything and everyone in it. If I win, you're dead, and that's good enough for me. I saw you shoot at the bar. You give me the draw."

X stroked Tanya's hair. "A duel. Hmmmmm..." X turned to LaPlace. "An amusing prospect. Draw up a contract under the new terms, Ken, as laid forth by John Wheelwright." X paused to tie up the loose ends. "My second will be in touch with you tomorrow to negotiate the details of our contest. This is agreeable to you."

John noticed that X never asked questions. "Until tomorrow," John whispered, and added, "Good day."

X gently tugged Tanya, who was studying John carefully, and led her back to the car. One of the X-men held the door of the Escalade open for Tanya, who sat delicately on the seat, still looking at John, letting her skirt ride up a bit and parting her fine legs tantalizingly wide, she slowly brought them together in front and arranged herself in the seat as the X-man slammed the door closed.

The enemy entourage reassembled in the same order that they arrived and sped away. Once they were out of sight, Alan let out a whoop and ran to John, but Grace got there first. Everyone cheered John enthusiastically except Arthur, who sat himself down on the steps with both hands pressing against his chest, breathing deeply, and smiling with eyes closed a blissful smile full of relief.

Sleep was fitful for all of them that night. Clouds had moved in from the big lake, and the warm air was being pushed out. The wind blew strong, and the drafty house gave them all a chill as they tossed and turned, each in their own world, considering what had happened and what was to come. Arthur's relief turning into sorrow, Alan's to anger, John's to fear, Andrea's to apprehension, Grace's to loving sympathy for her new man. Chris and Jalen? Out like a light.

8

The atmosphere at the farm wasn't so jubilant that next day, but the relief was still palpable. John spent most of the day in consultation with Alan, who would act as John's Second in the duel. Together they picked a Referee to represent them, worked out the wheres, whens, and hows of the upcoming contest, how far they would compromise on which parameters, and what particulars X's delegation might well insist upon for their own part.

Arthur realized that John had put his own life on the line to save his farm and dignity, and if he lost this duel that all would be lost indeed. John was their only hope, but he played all of this down to Arthur, assuring him that he could beat X in a fair contest. Privately, though, they wondered how much their confidence was shaped by the elation they all felt at the reprieve John had already earned for them. By evening, this elation was gone, and the real gravity of the situation was starting to press through.

It rained that cold, you're-lucky-it-ain't-snow-yet sort of rain that next evening, a reminder of the volatile capriciousness of the northern Michigan climate. The delegates trickled in slowly to Willy's. Alan was already there, and he waited in a booth near the pool tables for Mike Halloran, a family friend, who had agreed to take part in the referee function of the upcoming duel. Word had gotten out on the street almost immediately that X would appear in public to do what he did best, and the odds all over the territory were pretty steep against the unknown challenger. This promised to be the sporting event of the decade. X was out of town on business in the western U.P., so the duel would not take place for a few days at best.

Friday and Saturday were Rondayvoo, the biggest annual event in the Upper Peninsula. A giant flea market on 200 acres south of Marquette drew people from three states to peddle their wares. In addition to the usual mundane offerings, this was the best time to buy the guns, ammo, and related hi-tech accessories that the black market had to offer, and which were always in great demand. There would be unlimited alcohol and drugs of every description for those so inclined – BUY IN BULK, OR JUST ENJOY THE SHOW, one banner would announce. Sex was everywhere, and free as it ever gets, or at least relatively inexpensive.

There were contests of all sorts. Shooting, knife and ax-throwing, and the full-contact MegaMan contest that always resulted in a few fatalities were the biggest draws. There was even a beauty contest for Lady Superior that had but one event, the bikini display, by which the usually shivering young ladies would be judged. An atmosphere of almost total lawlessness prevailed at Rondayvoo. There were many fights, most harmless, but always at least a dozen deaths by all sorts of circumstances – not an event for the faint of heart. Law enforcement, and especially red helmets, were considered live targets. They stayed away. It was a No-Go Zone.

Alan ordered another beer and looked at his watch. Everybody, even his own man, was late. Typical. He stared idly at the gaggle of semi-nude ladies gossiping at the bar. Six nights a week, the ladies got to do their routines to live music, and this was a Live Music Night. The band wouldn't hit the stage till 9:30, but it already didn't look too promising. They were cowboys, natch, or at least costumed that way, and were taking full advantage of the half-price beer

and liquor prices which were one of the perks of being en-
tertainers at Willy's.

The place was nearly empty. There were the showgirls
and waitresses, two booths full of regulars, and a bespectacled fellow sitting by himself at one of the tables reading a
New York Times. Alan was, for no good reason, rather
suspicious of that guy. The door opened and in walked two
men, whom Alan didn't recognize as local X-men. They
walked back to Alan's booth.

"Hello," a darkly confident and direct young man in a
dark suit and leather coat addressed Alan. "You remember
me. I'm Skinner. The chess-player. You're Alan"

"That's right."

"Then we have a meeting. Is that right, Alan?"

"That's right." Alan motioned to the table next to him.
"Why don't we pull a couple of tables together so that everyone can be accommodated?"

This was done, and Alan ordered drinks for everyone
from a comically unattractive middle-aged waitress. In the
brief introductory small talk that followed, Skinner made it
clear that he was to act as Referee for X, and introduced a
bedraggled old fellow named Charley, who would be X's
Second.

The drinks arrived, but Alan was told when he tried to
pay the woman that his money was no good there and that
all their drinks were on the house. She stayed briefly to take
the just-arrived Mike's order. At length, the two Seconds
and the two Referees were settled with their drinks.

"Well," Alan suggested, "let's get down to business,
eh?"

Skinner rose from his seat and took off his full-length
tan leather coat. "Just a minute," he said, turned, and made
his way to the table of the bespectacled man. "Who are
you?" he inquired directly.

The man looked up from his paper. "Well, heh heh," he chuckled, tilting his chair back a bit on its rear legs as the big fellow loomed over him curiously. "I'm Stanley Nisbett. I'm from the *Sault Ste. Marie Daily News*," he smiled. "We heard about the uh, confrontation, coming up and, well, it's a good story, and I..."

"Beat it." Skinner cut him short.

"Just a couple of questions, and..."

"Get. The FUCK. Out. Of. The. Bar." Skinner enunciated clearly, moving closer to the reporter with each syllable, and ending up nose-to-frightened-nose when the chair crashed backward to the floor, spilling the hapless reporter to the dingy tiles. Everyone laughed heartily at the poor man, who rose and took hasty leave of Willy's, leaving his Times and a half-finished ginger ale on the table.

Skinner back at the table and the ice thoroughly broken, the four men began negotiations in easy earnest.

"Are we agreed on pistols?" Mike asked the forum. All consented. John would use his Custom Colt .45 Pistol; X would wield the Desert Eagle .50.

"You know, that gun had some problems," Alan noted. "I sort of figured X for something a little more... traditional."

"There's a guy in your neck of the woods named Aziz who made that gun a jewel," Skinner replied casually. "Out-of-the-box, it wasn't much. But man, I've seen what that gun can do with a little tender loving care."

"Yeah," Alan said. "Me too."

Skinner looked at Alan and laughed teasingly. "I understand you've already had a little demonstration."

"Well? How many bullets you gonna let 'em stuff in them things?" Charlie asked loudly, eager to join the youngsters in important conversation.

"Good point, Charlie," Skinner noted.

112

"Just one," offered Mike.

"I agree," said Alan. "If neither hits they ought to be too embarrassed to shoot again."

Skinner pondered this a bit. "Okay," he agreed. They consented that the magazines would be empty and checked by each Referee and that a single cartridge would be placed in each magazine by the shooter's Referee, and this process observed and checked by the opponent's Referee. That accomplished, each gun would be turned over to the shooter's Second, who would hand the gun to the duelist at his station. But what about the stations?

"25 yards," Alan offered, which is a condition that John all but demanded he secure in these negotiations.

"50 feet," countered Charley.

"15 yards sounds pretty good," Mike said.

"I was thinking of 30 feet," Skinner said with a smile.

They all looked at one another. "More drinks!" Mike proposed, an offer to which they all agreed heartily. The music started as the same uncomely waitress came to take their order. *A real one-two punch,* Alan thought to himself. Loud and distorted red-neck country music began booming from the band's antique speaker system. Skinner winced and rose. Mike wondered if another strong-arm tactic was about to unfold. Skinner followed the amplifier cords to the wall and yanked the plugs from their sockets.

"Hey man!" the lead singer whined into his dead microphone. Skinner went over to the fellow, reached into his pocket, and pulled out a wad of bills. He peeled off five $100 bills and distributed them among the band members with the stipulation that they would be each as quiet as a mouse until Skinner and his tablemates had left the bar. They agreed enthusiastically and ran to refill their glasses, but were waylaid by Willy, who said he wasn't going to pay them for the time they weren't playing. The ensuing argument was almost as loud and obnoxious as the music.

"God damn it," Skinner said as he returned to the table and sat. "Maybe we can get a little peace now." The waitress returned with a new round and departed. "Man, that is one butt-ugly woman," Skinner said quietly, and all except Charley laughed.

"Maybe you should give her a hundred dollars to put her shirt back on," Alan suggested.

More laughs here, but Charley was not amused. "I gotta pee," he rose to announce and ambled toward the men's room.

Skinner noticed Mike and Alan smiling at one another. "He's a character, alright," Skinner said, sipping his beer.

"Not the kind," Mike ventured, "somebody might expect X to pick for his Second."

Putting his bottle back down on the table, Skinner looked at Mike. "X took a shine to Charley years ago. Kinda protects him. Watches out for him. Now, Charley wants to watch out for X." Skinner looked thoughtful. "He's kinda like X's dog."

After a few minutes, the bathroom door creaked, and back sauntered old Charley.

"Where was we?" Charley demanded as he sat.

"Distance," Mike reminded. After considerable haggling, which Alan wondered whether or not was sincere, the 25-yard figure as put forth by Alan was accepted. He presumed, rightly, that this is what X wanted, too. They also agreed on six-foot diameter chalk circles in which the duelists must confine themselves once the Referees declared the duel ready to commence. The circles would be marked by Alan and Charley by 10 pm the night before the duel. This strange provision was specified by Alan and accepted by Skinner.

"When and where?" Mike asked the group.

"X won't be back until Thursday," Skinner thought aloud. "Friday and Saturday are Rondayvoo," he thought for a moment. "That leaves Sunday, or else during the Rondayvoo," he concluded and looked at his colleagues.

"How 'bout during Rondayvoo?" Alan offered.

"How 'bout Sunday?" Skinner countered.

This time, it was Alan's turn to make a pretense at hard negotiations. John had preferred Sunday, too. Alan was getting the hang of this game. Sunrise on Sunday morning was agreed upon.

"Well," Charley said, "we got the when and the how. Where we gonna do this at?"

"Not around here," Skinner said flatly.

"Not near Grand Marais, either," Mike countered. There was a general pause.

"How 'bout the Rondayvoo grounds?" Skinner offered. He scanned the faces of his rivals.

Alan sought the security of a mass audience outside of X's territory, not trusting X outside of public scrutiny. He leaned forward. "That's okay with us. With one condition," he looked closely at Skinner and Charley. "I want four riflemen, two of yours and two of ours, posted at the corners. If either duelist shoots before the Referees start the duel, or if they even so much as step outside the circle after the refs start the duel, the riflemen have the right to shoot the offender. And any attempt by X to draw first means that if X doesn't die by my brother's pistol, he dies by the riflemen. Also, John gets the draw."

"Absolutely not."

"Listen. X didn't object to that provision when it was offered to him, and X specified to his lawyer LaPlace that the terms of the duel be drawn up to the conditions indicated by John."

Genuine haggling followed this stipulation, and Alan did not give in. At length, Skinner and Charley agreed, not being able to logically refute the proposal.

Skinner drew up the papers, and Alan and Mike signed them. Skinner reached inside his coat and brought forth four new pieces of paper. He gave two to Alan, instructing, "Look at the first page."

"When X kills John," Skinner began reading, "he will take possession of the farm and dispose of the farm in any way he sees fit." He looked at Alan. "You do recognize these terms, don't you? This is what your brother specified. Correct?"

"That's right."

Skinner went back to the paper. "Since everyone in this territory is aware of the conditions of the duel, X believes that your father will consider it a manner of personal honor to surrender the farm as specified, and therefore expects the appropriate documents, deeds, surveys, and so forth, to be in order on the day after X kills your brother in the duel. A list of the required documents is appended on page two."

He paused and finished the rest of his beer in a long swallow. "Now. In the unlikely event of John killing X, well, we need not concern ourselves with this. The mere fact of X's unlikely demise would fulfill entirely your brother's expectations. Is this also correct?"

"Almost."

Skinner was startled. "That was the deal. What the hell is this 'almost' bullshit?"

"If John kills X, there shall be no attempt on his life in retribution."

Skinner considered this for a long minute. "Not that day," he said at last.

"Not ever."

"I can't promise that. Think about it. I don't know the future. I don't know what will happen in the long run. But I can promise if John kills X, he'll be safe for the day."

"And if not, then the deal's off and my family keeps the land and you all bugger the fuck off."

Skinner looked down at the table. Nodding, thinking. Alan's point was hard to refute. It was reasonable. He looked up. "Agreed."

"Good," Alan said. "Okay then. Add that and let me read it."

They had another round in silence while Skinner made the changes and additions to the second document. When he was finished he gave it to Alan to approve. It was all very succinct, easy to understand, with no legalese to make anybody nervous.

"I'm okay with this," Alan said after his careful read.

"Good. Take those two papers home and have your father and your brother sign them. They are to be returned tomorrow at 10 p.m., right here. I'll send someone by to collect them. If they aren't returned," he stood, "all bets are off." Charley rose also. Skinner offered his hand to Alan, who took it. "A pleasure meeting you," Skinner said, and shook Mike's hand, too. Charley followed suit.

The two X-men turned and walked toward the door. When they were halfway there, Mike called to him. "Hey, Skinner!" He stopped and turned. "How can you work for that guy?"

Skinner smiled. "I have a lot of money, a beautiful home, nice car, two months of vacation a year, work that's never boring, and I don't have to kill people. I don't like to, and it's not my job to."

Mike held Skinner's gaze and nodded. "I couldn't do it."

"You're not me, Mike. Good night."

9

Spirits around the Wheelwright farm remained optimistic and light that week. Everyone had a lot of faith in John as a shooter and were confident that he would be a match for X. Or at least, this was the attitude that John observed among his family and friends. John had not thought about the duel, but he wondered if X, for all that he knew of John's immediate past and activities, knew about his status as an Olympic shooter.

X's display of shooting prowess in the bar was most impressive. John recalled looking at the single ragged hole in the middle of the dart board, and he reckoned that it hung about the same 25 yards away as the specified dueling distance. He wondered how happy and confident everyone would be if they saw that?

He made love to Grace for the first time the night of the challenge, and it was as mindblowing as he had imagined it would be. They spent as much time together as they could manage. John convinced her that it would be a bad idea for her to go back to her little farm until the present crisis was over. She was safe with him, and she felt the same way. He had never felt toward any woman as he did toward Grace. The family liked her, too.

Jalen was having the time of his life. He had not lost a chess game since his arrival (except for the beating he took from Skinner, which everyone politely agreed would never be spoken of again). Toleration of black folks in this region was low, but no one dared treat Jalen poorly. The boy had been staying at Ty's place, and Ty, who had always thought of himself as the local chess champ, could never get more than 20 moves with Jalen before the boy crushed him. Ty, though fond of the youngster, was becoming obsessed with beating him and was driven to episodes of loud cursing and anger when Jalen would watch TV, read Sports Illustrated, and play chess with Ty at the same time, only to beat the poor man ragged, much to the amusement of Jean. Chris wanted to laugh at these episodes, too, but wisely thought better of it.

It had been three days since the challenge was made, and John had hardly seen anything of Chris. Tomorrow was the first day of Rondayvoo, and John wondered if the grey poet would go along with them. Chris spent a lot of time at Ty's place, cavorting with the saucy Jean, perhaps? Ty was no fool, but Chris, uncharacteristically, did a lot of work on Ty's place and was fast becoming an indispensable conversationalist for Ty, who was happy to have the mental stimulation. Jean had other virtues, but a stimulating conversationalist she wasn't. Was it possible, John wondered, that Ty turned a blind eye to Chris' frolics with his live-in maid? The thought made him laugh out loud.

"What's so funny?" Grace asked sleepily. She was lying with her head on John's shoulder and jostled awake.

"Chris and Jean," he chuckled.

"Mmmmmm..." Grace purred. "She likes him. He writes her poems."

"How do you know?"

Grace lifted her head a bit and smiled at John. "She tells everybody." She let her head sink back down on John's shoulder. "She's very proud of her poet."

"Oh man..." John sighed. "I hope Ty doesn't rip his heart out and make him eat it."

Grace pulled herself up to sit and made a face. "Gross." She stretched like a cat and yawned. "Ty wouldn't do that, would he?"

"*I* would."

119

She leaned over him so that her breasts hung free over his face, like luscious, ripe fruits. "That's a sweet thing to say," she whispered as he kissed her white breasts. Then she pulled away and made the face again. "I guess." And bounded up from the bed, eluding John's grab for her.

"Come back," he ordered playfully.

Grace grabbed her robe and pulled it on hurriedly. "I can't," she said as she opened the bedroom door and turned. "My period started."

She ran downstairs to make coffee, John hoped. He looked over to where his lover had lain and saw a few scarlet dots on the new sheet she had just bought in town for their bed. "Life with a woman," he said to the ceiling, staring at the cracks and thinking about the life he might have once the duel was over.

Everyone spent that Thursday preparing for Rondayvoo. John and Alan took another long swamp cruise during the afternoon while Grace went back to her farm to pick up some clothes and other effects to see her through the weekend. The Ohlssons were happy to watch the farm for her and wished her well in her romance with John Wheelwright, who was by now quite a celebrity. The rest of the friends and family enjoyed the return of the September sunshine, reveling in good conversation and recreation about the farm, which was still Arthur's.

That evening was characterized by more of the same massive feasting and partying that had gone on most nights since the prodigal son had returned. It was the wee hours now, and father and brothers knew they should get some sleep. Tomorrow they would head west to the Rondayvoo, and hangovers were not in the game plan. They would all camp in their trucks both nights, and on Sunday was the duel that the family hoped would end their problems. John was not so sure that this would be the case, and he didn't believe his father and brother were so confident either. X's reputation was so utterly loathsome that it was doubtful they would indeed be free from retribution even if John killed X at Sunday dawn, despite the written agreement.

Such thoughts were pushed from their minds with the help of good beer, the last of the case of wines that Grace brought, and some mighty fine homegrown reefer that Alan had grown on the farm and just recently harvested. His father disapproved of marijuana but had long accepted that most of the young folks indulged in the habit, and no harm seemed to come from it other than a lot of silliness, strange conversation, and an often empty refrigerator the next morning.

Alan was bringing John up to date with some of his, shall we say, formative experiences of his last six years. Alan had killed three men, two of them in self-defense. He had a reputation for toughness and coolness in the face of trouble, and only strangers dared bully the strong, skinny lad. He had by now developed, or rather adopted, a firm personal philosophy regarding the dispatching of others.

"Karma."

"Did you say 'karma'?" John asked.

"Ahhh, he's crazy with that bullshit," his father said, emptying the ashtray with the four big roaches in it into the messy trashcan, which he knew would annoy his sons, and then poured more beer from the pitcher into his glass. Arthur had a major buzz going – rare for him.

"I made a little rule that I would never shoot anybody, or hurt anybody seriously, if I was really pissed-off at them," Alan explained. "If I kill somebody, they goddam well had it coming. Two of those killings of mine were done ice-cold. No passion. If you indulge yourself, there's karma, and you'll pay for it one day; if you do it cold because it needs doin', then you're free."

"Like the old Samurai warriors," John said.

"Exactly!" Alan took a drink enthusiastically and wiped his chin. "Remember that book we read when we were kids?" The brothers laughed at the memory of the shared paperback, which John had gotten new and Alan enjoyed dog-eared years later. Arthur was so happy sitting with his sons like this after so many years. He was proud of how they turned out, and he missed his wife keenly.

"That one Samurai guy, remember him?" Alan said, "that the Emperor sent to kill a guy, and when he found him, the guy spat in the Samurai's face? It pissed him off so much that he put his sword away and refused to kill him."

"That was the best story," John recalled. "And then the next day, when he found the guy, he spit in his face again, but the samurai just wiped it off,"

"And chopped his head off,"

"IN ONE STROKE!" the brothers hollered in unison, quoting the last line of the story, and they laughed hysterically.

The old kitchen clock said almost 3:00, but no one was tired. Everyone enjoyed another glass of beer, the last of Ty's homemade brew.

"You never killed in anger?" John asked.

"Once."

"Harry Barber," his dad remembered.

"The neighbor?! Holy shit," John said. "Harry Barber was a crazy son of a bitch ten years ago. What'd he do for you to kill him?"

"Said I was poaching on his land."

"Were you?"

"I was *walkin'* on the *edge* of his land. Came out cursing with his shotgun leveled on me, which is already a good reason to shoot somebody. Killed Ruff, you remember, Mike's dog, with it. I was watching his dog for the weekend. Great dog-sitter, eh? Standin' right next to me. Blew his little doggie head clean fuckin' off. I couldn't believe it! Andrea was with me. Jesus Christ, she was only 13!" Alan remembered all this like it was yesterday. "He moved the barrel toward Andrea, probably just clumsy but who knows, and, naturally, goddamn it, I shot him."

"Sounds like a righteous shoot to me," John offered.

"To me, too, goddamn it," their father chimed in. "I don't know why it bothers him."

"I gut shot him," Alan said flatly. "That's why. I could have killed him quick, but instead I shot him in his big ugly belly. Sonofabitch laid there twistin' around and screamin' and moanin'... shit." Alan took a drink.

"Had it coming, sounds like," John offered.

"No. I stared at him for about ten seconds, I don't know how long, enjoying his suffering because of what he did to Ruff. And man, I *deeply* enjoyed it. Andrea was too scared to even cry. But then it hit me, and I felt like a goddamn monster. I felt dirty. I put one in his head and he went quick."

Alan's head sank and, bleary-eyed with smoke and drink, he stared vacantly at the space between his boots. "I'm gonna have to pay for those ten seconds one of these days."

Reaching over, Arthur hugged his son's shoulder. "Bullshit, Alan. You're only human. You're not going to be punished because you're not perfect."

Alan looked up at his dad, then over at John, who was grinning. They all laughed.

The room spinning a bit, Arthur said his goodnights, and atypically hugged each of his boys in a long, tight embrace before climbing the stairs to bed, wiping tears of tipsy joy from his eyes.

The brothers stayed up a while to roll and smoke one more, totally unnecessary, joint before retiring themselves, knowing that a hangover was inevitable, but that tonight it was worth it.

In contrast to the party atmosphere which prevailed at the Wheelwright farm, The Palace was quiet this Thursday night. All the courtiers and hangers-on were preparing for their trip to Rondayvoo, and X had made it known that he required some peace and quiet this night. His investigations into the past of John Wheelwright had finally uncovered his Olympian past, and though X was supremely confident in the perfection of his own shooting skills, he was not comfortable with the fact that his usual bulwark of advantages was not in place.

He sat in his office in his big leather La-Z-Boy recliner, enjoying cognac and a Cuban cigar, blowing smoke rings and putting the final touches on his strategy for victory on Sunday morning. His view from the master suite on the third floor of the massive old mansion was spectacular. It was almost 9:30, and the moon was just peeking up over the horizon. Obtaining the house and securing for his own the thousands of acres which surrounded his Palace was a messy business, but at times like this, he knew it was worth it. Despite a rocky and poor youth, life had been good to Xavier Blount.

The cigar, which X had not really craved, was employed to cover the strong fragrance that one or the other of Tanya's new guests was wearing, and which X thought revolting. Tanya liked to handpick ladies for the mutual enjoyment of Xavier and herself, but Tanya's appetite for the local women was causing X some problems. He had not revealed this to Tanya, for having finally found a woman worthy to be his consort, he was not eager to evince any weaknesses nor deny her anything she desired. To her credit, she chose well, and most of the women were easily seduced at $1,000 a visit, plus tips. These were hard times. But even the awful consequences of incurring X's wrath and the massive cash payments to the ladies whom Tanya favored were sometimes not enough to sufficiently intimidate the families of some of these women, who were not amused by the recruitment of their daughters, sisters, wives, even mothers, for such purposes. X had been quick to quell any and all serious protestations among the local families so affected, but he thought this a serious waste of resources, and unnecessarily injurious to his already shaky public relations.

But it was worth it. His mind drifted back to the time he first saw Tanya, who was then engaged to a business partner in Quebec. This man was impossibly rich, but he bored her. At that time, she spoke Russian fluently, French passably, and English not at all, but the electricity that passed between Tanya and X at their first encounter made speech superfluous. X had made the trip to solidify relations with this man, who not only ran a large drug trade but owned a fleet of ships. X had become the most important distributor for his operation, and so essential to the success of his enterprise in America that he was powerless to object when X took Tanya away with him to live among the pines in the forests of Lake Superior. That was a year ago, and he had not regretted for a moment making this imaginative and glamorous woman his consort. X feared only one thing in life: that Tanya would become bored. So, he did everything in his growing power to satisfy her every whim.

The master bedroom door opened, and Tanya, still fully-clothed, led one of her playmates by the hand into X's chambers. She was completely naked and not more than sixteen. Her initial nervousness was moderated by some of the narcotics which Tanya administered in certain situations such as this. The slim redhead had a dreamy look but retained enough girlish modesty to try to shield herself from the eyes of X, who admired her from his chair. She gave him a misty smile.

"Isn't she adorable, Xavier?" Tanya asked proudly. "Look here," she said as she turned the girl around and patted her smooth bottom.

"What's your name, my dear?" X asked the girl.

"Karen," she turned and answered in a small voice.

"And tell me, Karen," X continued, "do you mind being here with us tonight?"

"No," she grinned. "Nobody knows I'm here."

"And she has been well rewarded for sharing her charms," Tanya said sweetly, "haven't you, darling?"

"Yes."

X knew how Tanya worked the young ones. Every request the girl complied with, Tanya would reward with a little cash. As her demands became increasingly exotic, Tanya would increase the reward until the allotted $1,000, and Tanya herself, were both quite exhausted.

"We're getting lonesome all alone in that big bed, aren't we, darling," Tanya cooed to her debutante as she led her to a chair across from X. "Sit here." The girl sat with crossed ankles and half-closed eyes. Tanya knelt in front of the girl, gripped her knees, and spread them apart and upward, draping her pretty legs over opposite arms of the chair. Tanya moved a bit to the side so that X could enjoy the view, and slowly raked the inside of Karen's thighs with her long, perfect fingernails, making pale white streaks on the girl's flushed, pink thighs. Karen moaned softly and swayed her head back and forth languidly. "Come visit us, Xavier," Tanya called to X.

But X had work to do, and for all the enticements set before him, he knew that business always took precedence over pleasure. It was one of the secrets of his success.

"I'm afraid I must decline this evening, my dear," X stood and stretched. Tanya pouted, but X knew that she was quite capable of salvaging a fulfilling evening on her own. On his way out of the room, he grabbed his notebook and smiled a goodbye to the ladies.

X's office suite was large and well-equipped with the latest computers, monitoring, and telecommunications equipment. He sat at a station and typed a brief message, paging two of his most capable captains. He awaited their arrival with more cognac, while he put the finishing touches on a plan that would restore his advantages, assuring four times over that his victory on Sunday would be a shoe-in.

The requested men arrived within minutes, and the alerted staff expedited their passage to the office, where they paid their respects and took a seat, awaiting orders.

One of the men was Skinner Sorenson, and if it could be said that Xavier Blount trusted a human being, Skinner would be the one. Next to him sat Whit Campbell, a mastermind of mayhem. Whit was called upon only in the rarest of occasions when delicate ingenuity and brute force were required to get a job done. X opened a cabinet and took down two crystal snifters. He went back to his desk and sat, offering cigars to the men, who declined.

"John Wheelwright won a Silver Medal in the Olympics six years ago for pistol shooting," X told his men. "Perhaps

I should have killed him on the spot, and his whole family with him on that farm of theirs. I know that most of my captains are of that opinion." He glared at the two men for a few seconds and then moved his gaze out through the big office window. "On reflection, I'm glad that a massacre was avoided. I need that land *legally*. And if the idea of a duel pleases my lady, then I am not averse to the sport and consider the matter trivial."

X poured cognac for the two captains. "But upon learning of my opponent's secret skill with pistols, I believe that he is playing a sort of game with me." The two men retrieved their glasses. Eyes on his boss, Skinner pressed his face to the snifter and breathed the heady bouquet of Extra Old Champagne Cognac. X continued. "I see treachery here and have therefore decided to take steps of my own to admonish John Wheelwright for his presumptions, and to assure myself an *easy* victory."

X held his glass up to the others as if to make a toast. "In my plan," he said, "there is a scuffle, a raid, and men in the trees." Glasses clinked, and the men drank deep.

10

No one remembered anything like it. Every year the law had tried to stop it, but it just kept getting bigger. This year, there seemed to be more of everything – people, noise, booths and tables and tents, food, drink and drugs, sex, and guns. This year's Rondayvoo was the biggest ever.

All the Wheelwrights had a shopping list for the long-awaited occasion. When it came to guns, night-vision, re-loading supplies, and the like, there was no reason to buy anywhere else. Prices were good, and the bartering was frantic.

John, fighting off a monstrous hangover, was looking for a replacement for his old and beloved AR-15, stolen by the good citizens of Philadelphia. He was astonished at the high prices these models demanded and decided to wait until next year. Those new red-dot optics for his .45 looked nice, though...

His brother had saved his pennies all year and was at a tent where a couple of characters were selling Night Optics Scopes for a fraction of the price of other merchants. It was impolite to ask why, but it was becoming clear that these boys needed to sell out quickly and disappear. *Stolen*, Alan thought, *but what the hell?* He shelled out $600 for the scope and case, new-in-box, but there was no bargaining. "Hey pal, these things are $2,500, right?" the man had told him. "If you don't buy it for my price, I'll sell it to some other lucky sonofabitch in five minutes, you unnerstand, dontcha?" Alan understood and made his purchase.

"No receipt?" he twitted the man, who laughed as he stuffed the bills into his pants.

Grace and Andrea were entirely caught up in the festivities, sticking close to the brothers, but checking out hot guys, various tents, and displays. There was no organization here. One might find a table with hand-made baby quilts sandwiched between dealers in demolition supplies. Grace, John thought uncomfortably, was spending a lot of time looking at those baby quilts.

Chris took turns with Jalen pushing Ty around in his wheelchair, and Arthur and Jean blazed a trail through the crowds. Ty was trying the old hair-of-the-dog hangover cure, but Arthur was sickened by the sight of beer that early afternoon and the noise and smells of the event were a little oppressive to him, though he kept this to himself (as he invariably did) as they perused the offerings.

A few hundred yards north, the shooting contests had started, but by now, there were few among the crowd who did not know about the real shooting contest scheduled for Sunday morning. The betting was formal, and business was brisk. John enjoyed watching the odds, which were running seven-to-one in favor of X. He was invited, and even rather rudely challenged a couple of times that day, to enter some of the pistol events. He refused. He was the main event, and he well knew it.

Alan and John stopped by the MegaMan contest area, which was always the most popular event. Set up like a boxing ring, the floor was grass, and the rules were simple: make your opponent surrender or knock him unconscious. There were no weight classes nor pads, nor helmets. Neither was there a time limit, one round was allotted with no breaks for any reason. In the ring, one could find a wrestler pitted against a kickboxer, or a traditional boxer wrangling with a judo expert. As long as you were registered by noon of the first day of Rondayvoo, you had a place on the roster, no questions asked. There was no entry fee for contestants, but spectators paid $20 a visit. From a field of 64 contenders, it would be whittled down to just two men by tomorrow night. The winner would walk away with $10,000, and, keeping with the spirit of the event, there was no second prize.

The brothers laid down their money and managed to get a seat in the back. (The seats were superfluous, though, as everybody stood to best see the action.) In the ring were two men in karate uniforms. One was dressed ostentatiously in a black uniform with many colorful patches representing who-knows-what. This fellow had a gold and black belt with seven stripes and his name blazoned along the back. He warmed up with a few spectacular kicks accompanied by loud yells.

The other guy was much smaller than his opponent, had a plain white uniform with a plain black belt. He stood quite still in his corner, waiting for the bell. When it finally sounded, the big colorful guy made the sign of the cross and came running out of his corner at his opponent. He stopped a few feet in front of him and did a spin kick aimed at the smaller man's head. In a flash, this man pulled his head back, grabbed the foot of the man as it passed by his face, and with the heel of his free hand, he pounded the man's outstretched leg on his kneecap, making a sickening snapping sound. He then snapped a powerful kick to the exposed groin of his opponent, who crumpled to the grass in a sustained shriek of pain. The match took less than five seconds.

John and Alan looked at each other, wide-eyed in amazement. "Holy shit!" Alan hollered to John over the appreciative yelling of the crowd. "Did you see that?"

Yes, it was quite a show. The brothers watched in amazement five more confrontations, each spectacular in its own way. They made a mental note to return tomorrow night for the final rounds, if they could afford the $50 admission. The tickets jumped to $100 for the final match, and it was always a capacity crowd.

There were two amenities that the organizers of the Rondayvoo had provided: a place to take garbage, and about a hundred porta-johns. There was no security, no assigned sleeping spaces (folks slept in their trucks or out in the open), and only a small area was set aside for campers. The noise never ceased. Laughter and gunfire was the rule at all hours, and it was amazing (except for a few accidents and the odd murderous outburst) how a spirit of cheerfulness and goodwill ruled these days of the Rondayvoo.

The X-men were everywhere, and each month Alan had noticed that more and more of his acquaintances were joining the Organization. Jobs were few up here and money tight, but those who had the right stuff could become well-off in the service of Xavier Blount. The X-men had never interfered in the doings at Rondayvoo, as it was a little west of X's influence, and considered an almost sacred event by everyone in the U.P.

They all met for an early dinner in the food sector, deciding together on a barbecue that looked good. They sat in a tent at a long table, under a hastily-painted sign that announced -

FRED & LUCY
Hot 'N Jucy
Texas Bar-B-Q

-- and waited for chicken and ribs while enjoying pitchers of beer. John felt better after the food but hoped that Grace would not want to drag him over to the pavilion where the music and dancing had begun. John was not keen on dancing but knew that Andrea was, and Andrea, he knew, would try to get Grace to go with her. Strangely, it was Ty who made the suggestion.

"Hey! Let's go over and watch the girls dance, whaddaya say?" Only John and Alan, who moaned loudly at the suggestion, thought it was a bad idea, but they knew the character of Rondayvoo at night and were not going to let these two attractive ladies go without them, where they would be as chunks of meat to wolves.

"You know, you don't have to come along," Grace said to the reluctant brothers on the walk to the Pavilion. John looked at Alan.

"Yeah, right."

They were stopped on the way by two men who singled John out for conversation. "Hey you!" yelled the drunkest of the pair, who was still wearing his sunglasses though the sun had set almost a half-hour earlier. "You're John Wheelwright, right?" He cackled and turned to his friend. "Wheel wright, right?" he laughed at his clever rhyme. Then suddenly turning back on John, the man whipped his coat to one side revealing a Colt Single Action Army in a new and ornate holster, probably just purchased. He stood there, wobbling a little. "So, you're the big shot shooter, eh?"

Alan had a sneaky hand on his Browning Hi-Power, in a small-of-the-back holster, but John was less concerned. Family and friends moved off to the side and stood watching in various degrees of apprehension.

"Listen pal," John said calmly, his hands open to his side. "Don't do this. Just move on and enjoy the night, huh?"

"I ain't goin' NOWHERE," the drunken desperado declaimed as the side-to-side wobble took on a front-to-back aspect, and the fellow fell face-forward into the wet dirt.

"Sorry," his friend said as he tried to rouse the fallen gunslinger. "He's just really drunk, y'know?"

Laughing with relief and appreciation of the comedy, they made their way at last to the pavilion where a country-western band dressed like bikers played their music to a throng of enthusiastic dancers. Chris wanted to dance the night away with Jean, but was wary of the wheelchair-bound Ty. Chris had been a good guest at Ty's place, and the enjoyment of company was mutual.

But did Ty know about last night after he went to sleep, how Jean met Chris out in the garden, and how they made love right there, crushing the late-season herbs with their bodies, their fragrance mingling with the scent of the lovers? *Hmmm*, Chris pondered, *gotta be a poem in there.*

Though in general the thought made Chris nervous, Ty's friendly attitude toward him never varied. He had an idea. He went over to the little table where John and Grace sat with Alan and Andrea. Jalen was under the table, playing hide-and-seek with a few noisy kids who sped by yelling, not seeing Jalen in his hiding place.

"Grace, would you like to dance?" Chris said in a comically exaggerated gesture of chivalry.

"Yes, I would," she rose and curtsied and affected a southern-belle accent, "Thank yew fer askin', sir."

"Nothin' wrong with dancing with your sister, you know!" Arthur called out from a nearby table where he sat with Ty and Jean.

The brothers were struck dumb in horror by this suggestion, and Andrea was insulted. "I don't want to dance with these, these, bastards," she yelled back to Arthur, trying to make her small voice heard over the music. The old folks had a laugh.

"Excuse me, but I'd love to dance with you."

A clean-cut young man about Andrea's age, whom the brothers did not recognize stood next to the table, waiting for Andrea's response. She rose and smiled at the fellow and took off with him to the dance floor. Just like that. John and Alan looked at one another blankly and sipped their beers.

The man was Terry Kimball, and he was a proud new member of X's organization, hand-picked for the job at hand. Kimball was an untrustworthy braggart who had clamored for years that X must be a real moron not to want him on board. A petty thief from St. Ignace, not even others of his ilk had a kind word for him. But the swaggering Kimball was considered a 'useful idiot.' He was thus perfect for this duty.

The song was over, and Chris brought Grace back to the table. "Where's Andrea?" he asked. His plan was to dance with Grace and Andrea, then cut a rug with Jean. Who could object?

John and Alan pointed to the far end of the dance floor, and Chris squinted through his thick glasses to see Andrea talking to a fellow, waiting for the next song to begin. Jean called Chris over to the grown-ups' table, and it was decided that a stroll to the bar was in order.

The brothers sat with Grace and kept a jealous eye on their little sister. She looked good in a crisp white blouse and a loose blue skirt with flowers printed on it, which hung a bit above the knee. Her legs were thin and tan, and she wore white ankle socks. The music started up again, and the three sat admiring Andrea the Dancer. Grace tried again to convince John to dance, but he remained stony against the idea.

Grace was getting into a snit. "Are we going to have some fun tonight, or are you just going to play chaperone?"

John sat up and forward and craned his neck to keep an eye on the dancers, but it was Alan who spoke his thoughts. "He's gettin' a little personal, ain't he?"

"Maybe she likes him," Grace said with some antagonism. "Maybe she actually is trying to *enjoy* herself."

The band started a slow song and the fellow put his arms around Andrea's waist, she about his neck. The brothers stood for a better look.

"What the hell is the matter with you guys?" Grace demanded.

"Just a second, Grace." John dismissed her. There was a small circle clearing around the dancing pair, and many people seemed to be laughing at the two dancers. John could see nothing irregular, but something was not right. Alan sensed it too.

"Let's go see what's goin' on," Alan suggested. Without even asking Grace to accompany them they stepped from the table but stopped in their tracks. They had seen the couple turn around and noticed that Andrea's partner had gathered her skirt up around her waist, exposing her skimpy underpants to the sniggering faces of onlookers. Andrea, of course, was oblivious to this rudeness.

John and Alan broke into a run, bashing dancing couples from their path. They reached their target simultaneously and smashed the dancer to the ground. Before they could properly discipline the offender, they were themselves set upon by two tables full of men who subdued the brothers. While Alan fought to escape from the stranglehold of three big men holding him down on the ground, he watched as three others dragged the thrashing John to a nearby table. The dancer struggled to pull the Ek Model 5 from John's belt while another man held John's arm down onto the wooden table. The dancer raised the knife and slammed it down into the back of John's right hand, tacking it securely to the table.

John, Alan, and the horrified Andrea screamed in unison as the stiff blade hit its mark. Alan wiggled a hand loose and worked at the butt of his concealed pistol, working it free and bashing one of the men on the nose, knocking him back. The dancer worked furiously at the knife handle but still could not pull it free from John's hand. Alan pulled loose, and when the others saw the gun, they drew back. Alan fired a single shot into the side of the dancer, who had just freed the knife from the bloody hand of John, screaming in agony as the knife was twisted out. At the shot, everyone stood away and pulled their guns, and Alan noticed that Arthur and Jean were also present by now, both wielding the revolvers that they had the foresight to bring along. Alan and Grace ran to John to assess the damage.

The dancer was dead. With at least ten guns drawn and pointed, Chris wheeled Ty into view, who had his Ruger at the ready. Chris had the small .38 Special that Ty was teaching him to use. The crowd disbursed at the sight of the guns, and even the bandstand emptied.

Arthur told Andrea to snap out of it and get the truck. Jean and Grace went for the other trucks. Guns drawn, the men looked at one another in tense silence, which Alan broke.

"Who are you sonsabitches?" he asked the general assembly. "You're X-men, aren't you. You fucking assholes," he hissed. "I'll remember every one of you sonofabitches."

The largest and best dressed of the pack put his pistol away and told the others in his gang to do the same. "I don't know what you're talkin' about," he said to Alan, who was shaking with rage. "One of our boys was just havin' hisself a little dance, is all. We don't know nothin' about X.

We was just defendin' our own. Now, why don't you folks put those guns away." He looked at Alan. "You killed a man, fella."

"Fuck you, you sonofabitch. I know who you all are."

Wheelwrights and friends joined the X-men in putting up their guns and waited, about ten minutes, until Jalen could be rounded up and all three trucks were on the scene. Jean, Ty, and Jalen loaded first. "We'll meet at Marquette General," Ty said.

Chris, Andrea, and Arthur took another truck, while Alan and Grace helped John into his truck. "You drive, Grace," he whispered to her. "And when I say go, you go." Alan got in on the passenger side and slammed the door, hoping that its dysfunctional lock would not ruin the maneuver he had planned. He instructed the two other trucks to go ahead.

"Hey, you," Alan spoke to the man he saw hold down John's arm. "Bring me John's knife on the ground over there. Or are you assholes knife thieves, too?"

The man glanced at the group's leader, who nodded consent. He bent to pick up the knife, wiping the blood from the blade on his filthy jeans as he approached the truck. With one hand, Alan took the wrist of the man, pulled him forward, and with his other arm encircled his neck in a tight grip. "GO!" he yelled to Grace, and the truck spun away, ripping up the turf to the sound of pistol shots which did not find their mark in the ducking passengers.

Alan held the man tightly until they had reached the highway, where they found the other two trucks waiting on the roadside. The dangling man's ankles were broken in transit, and he had been shot by one of his own men in the lower belly. Alan dropped the man in a heap. Arthur got out of his truck, calmly walked to the man and kicked him in the face, hard. Alan restrained his father.

"Look," he steadied Arthur, who was blind with the fury of revenge. "I'll take care of this guy. You gotta take John to the hospital. Not Marquette, either. They think we're going there. You take him to Escanaba. Okay?" He waited. "Okay?"

His father finally looked at Alan. "Okay."

"Take Grace, too. I'll see you at home."

They sped away, and Alan loaded the groaning man into the front seat. "We're going for a ride," he said to the terrified X-man and pulled away. He drove about five miles until he came to a two-track lumber road which ran through the pines. He took it. A couple of miles later, he pulled off to the side of the road and roughly unloaded his passenger. In addition to the broken ankles and, probably, feet too, the belly wound looked very bad, and his burst nose suffered the imprint of Arthur's boot. Alan had to work fast.

"Please take me to the hospital," the man panted pathetically.

"Yeah, sure," Alan chuckled. "Tell you what. You co-operate, and maybe I'll take you to the hospital, Okay?"

The man sang like a canary. X had put them up to it. He wanted John hurt. Alan took out the Ek No.5 that had minutes ago crippled his brother. "I already know that," Alan said, and slammed the knife into the man's hand. He howled in pain and cried hysterically as Alan twisted the knife free. Alan stood up and stretched, sauntered to the truck and opened the door, put John's Ek on the seat, took a Hershey bar from the glove-box, unwrapped it casually and took a bite.

"Why don't you tell me something I *don't* know, hmm?" he said, chewing the chocolate.

The man started spilling his guts every way he could. Alan was supposed to kill Kimball, just as he did. X would strike in revenge for Kimball's death. And there was going to be a sniper at the duel in case John shot X.

"Who?" Alan asked.

"I don't know," he whimpered.

Alan tugged at the man's ear and sliced it off in one smooth snick. "John keeps a sharp knife, eh?" he said to the man as he threw the severed ear into his lap.

The man screamed in absolute horror at the sight and passed out. Alan slapped him silly until he came to.

"Who's the sniper?"

"DON'T YOU THINK I'D TELL YOU IF I KNEW!!" he screamed uncontrollably.

Alan was convinced that the song was over. He took out his Hi-Power and put a bullet through the man's temple.

With one stroke X had removed an embarrassment to his organization, injured John Wheelwright beyond hope of quick recovery, and had a 'reason' to retaliate against the killing of Kimball and now this other man, for all knew that such retribution was standard behavior in this neck of the woods. There was one more thing. The man Alan killed only knew about one of the two snipers that X would post the day of the duel.

11

John picked up the piece of paper that the surgeon gave him and read from it to his brother. "*Semi-lunar* and *os magnum.*" He threw the paper to the floor.

"What's a semiloonar and dosmagnem?" Alan asked.

John struggled to sit up in bed and cradled his heavily bandaged right hand. "Those are the two bones that the knife went between." The bandage looked like a big white balloon wrapped in an Ace bandage. "Could have been worse, I guess."

"Is it gonna heal?"

"Not for a while." He looked at his brother. "Not in time, that's for sure." He looked away and closed his eyes with the pain of movement. "The surgeon at Escanaba thought it would heal all right, but that it would sometimes get stiff and cramp up a lot." Grace breezed into the bedroom and in her hand was a little glass vial half-full of milky-white beads.

"Open up," she ordered. John opened his mouth and Grace poured in a few pellets. "There."

"What's this?" John asked suspiciously.

"Arnica," she answered, ignoring his smirk.

"What time is it?" the groggy John inquired of Grace.

"A little before noon."

He looked to Alan sharply. "Any trouble last night?"

"None. Not a sound. We were on guard all night. Didn't even see anything."

"By this time tomorrow, the duel will be over," John said without emotion. Grace became angry.

"How can you shoot a gun like that!" She turned to Alan. "How can he shoot like that?" Alan looked away. Grace waited for an answer. "Well?"

"Look," John softly said to his lover, "there's no way out of this. If I don't fight tomorrow, then X will take the farm. Maybe worse. Probably worse. Somebody's got to face him."

"Dad sent Andrea away," Alan said to John. "She put up a big fuss, but she went. He drove her to Ironwood to see Aunt Milly as soon as he left you at the hospital."

"Good. Smart man."

"Nobody else will go," Alan continued. "Not Chris or Jean, not even Jalen."

"Are you going to shoot left-handed?" Grace was still dumbfounded that John would duel in this condition.

John looked at Alan, and they both smiled. He raised his balloon-bandaged hand and looked at Grace. "Well, I guess so, honey."

"Do you know how? Don't you need to practice or something?" She started to cry.

John pulled her over to sit next to him on the bed. "No. You see, it's like studying for an IQ test, Grace," he patted her hand. "Yeah, I can shoot left-handed."

"As good," Grace sniffed and wiped her eyes, "as with your right?" She looked into his eyes for the real answer, which John did not give her.

"Better, sometimes," John laughed and stood up. "I need to get dressed. How about giving me a hand, huh Grace?"

Alan ran downstairs to relieve Arthur and take the noon-to-4 watch. The mood around the farm was gloomy and anxious, though everyone did their best to hide it. It was a misty rain that fell all that day, and friends and family passed the hours inside reading, preparing for the morning, napping, or just sitting quietly. They all had to leave for the duel by 5:30 in the morning to get to the grounds by sunrise.

Jalen spent most of that day buried deep in the chess-books that Skinner gave him. He slammed his little palm onto the book and whispered, "So that's how he did it!"

"Did what?" John asked, siting cuddled up with Grace on the sofa.

Jalen didn't answer for almost half a minute then blurted loudly, *"I'm gonna kill that Skinner son-of-bitch!"*

"HEY!" Grace cried.

"Whoa, Jalen, chill there buddy," John added.

The boy looked up, shocked at the reprimand. "Did I say that out loud?"

"You sure did," John replied.

"I'm sorry," Jalen said. "I only meant I would kill him with my chess."

"Whatever it takes," John joked. Grace glowered.

Chris spent part of the afternoon writing poetry in the library wing of the farmhouse and had just put the finishing touches on a little ode to his paramour. He called to Jean, whisked her into the room and shut the door.

"Hi sweetie," she kissed him on the cheek. "What's up?"

"Ummm," he handed her the half-sheet of paper, "this here's for you," he said clumsily, but Jean heard only music. "Hope you like it." She read:

How, across the minutes and years that turn us old
can I turn back?
A one-way road with stillness at the finish ...
Some walk, some run, others pushed, but
I stop, and see
You, a golden vintage,
and a grizzled and timeworn me.
The minutes and years that turn us old

can turn us back again if fortune smiles.
Can heal a wound so long suffered that we thought we
were the wound.
Can make a passion we dared not admit again
bloom again.
Rain to snow and ice and back again to gentle showers –
I know this road better now.
I am new and strong,
and younger than I am.
Love,
Chris

Jean kissed Chris passionately, gratefully. She suggested that they go for a walk in the gentle rain, into the woods, where Jean would reward her poet abundantly for his labors.

John was ready for duty when his time came at 7:00 that night. He was urged to get some rest, but he brushed off their pleas, maintaining that there was no way that sleep would come this night. Ty and Alan came inside; John and Chris would take their turn until 10:00. Everyone was tired, and though Chris looked particularly weary and beat he was not willing to let someone stand his watch for him. These days had been quite an adventure for the poet, and he was determined to prove that he could carry his load as well as any of the other men.

John chose a Browning semi-auto shotgun from Arthur's arsenal, the only gun he felt comfortable with shooting one-handed. Chris had one of the Mini-14s but practiced most of the time with the little pistol that Arthur had given him, and to which he had taken quite a shine.

"How you doin' on that .38 Special?" John asked Chris on the way out the door.

"I'm a by sure as shootin' one hell of a quickshot sum-bitch," Chris said in his best bad western accent. John laughed and pointed to the weeds behind the house.

"You get on that side of the house, and I'll be on this side about 100 yards away – same deal as a couple of nights ago. Dad and Alan are upstairs, and Grace and Jean and Ty are downstairs. They're armed and awake." He tapped Chris' chest with his good index finger. "There's a high probability of unpleasantness tonight, so keep sharp."

Kneeling in the weeds, the sun down, the rain gone, John was beginning to feel a chill, which he recognized was not from the evening air. He could no longer push the duel from his mind, and the thought of the morning descended upon his soul like a dark shroud. He shivered and thought of Grace. If he hadn't met her it wouldn't be so bad. If he had a future, he realized with a stab of affection, it was her. His hand hurt like a son of a bitch, but he dared not take the opioid pills he was given. He needed to stay sharp.

Neither Grace nor his family had talked to John directly about the duel. They were worried and afraid, but they were careful not to show it. Optimism reigned on the surface. No one even made plans about what to do if John were killed tomorrow. Maybe, he thought, they had made plans but did not want to undermine his confidence by telling him about them. Maybe he should have thought of a back-up plan for them.

What the hell... this sort of thinking was useless and harmful, and just the sort of thinking that rat bastard X was probably wishing John was doing, and here he was doing it. He tried to clear his mind, but pain tugged at his body and sadness tugged on his soul, dragging it down.

Time crawled by. It was about 9:45 and all had remained quiet. Maybe he would try to get some sleep after all. He was about to stand and stretch when he heard it. It came from along the road on the north side of the farm. He heard the muffle of footsteps in the gravel. Chris was not far from this activity, and John hoped that he had picked up on it. John crawled through the weeds noiselessly and slowly toward the other side of the house. It appeared that X would indeed try to extract a measure of revenge before the duel, adding another layer of suffering to bury even deeper John's slim hopes for victory.

By the sound of it, John guessed three, maybe four men along the road. He had supposed that they would come to the clearing and head for the front of the house, but they didn't. Instead, he could hear them making their way through the bushes and weeds. John realized in a panic that they were going to come around to the rear of the house and that they would have to go through Chris to do it. "He's not cut out for this shit," John whispered to himself as he hastened his crawl as much as he dared.

They stopped. Had they heard him? Had they heard Chris? Tense moments passed and then John heard a sound that turned his guts to water. *Chris had begun to snore.*

John was still about 75 yards away and well out of shotgun range. To his horror, he saw one of the men (John discerned three altogether) split from the crouched group and make his way toward the snoring Chris. John's mind raced. The man was almost upon him. John up and ran and screamed "CHRIS!" at the top of his lungs when at the same moment he heard the shot he was dreading. The two other men rose, and John shot the Browning in their direction, at least 60 yards away. They fell back a bit and returned fire. John fell to the weeds again, and to his relief, heard gunfire opening up from the house. He turned and looked. Upstairs and downstairs windows were blazing gunfire at the retreating men. They were all hit and down.

In a few moments, Arthur and Alan ran past him through the weeds to the fallen men. John rose and yelled at them.

"GET DOWN!" and father and brother hit the dirt as one. "There's another one over here. Cover me." And John made his way toward the hapless Chris. He heard a stirring a few yards away. "You're surrounded. Give up," John ordered.

"It's me."

"*Chris!*" John leaped to his feet and went to his friend. There the greybeard sat, spattered with blood, and next to him was another man, obviously dead, with a hole in his chest still bleeding copiously.

John spun. "It's Chris!" he called to the men. "He's okay." John heard crying and turned to see Grace hugging Jean, who wept with relief that Chris was alright. John looked back down at Chris.

"I killed him. Didn't I?" Chris was in shock.

"You sure did, buddy," John smiled at his friend. "You shot him with that silly pop-gun, didn't you? Well... not so silly, I guess, after all."

"I must've fallen asleep," he said tonelessly, staring straight ahead. "He woke me up. And came at me and the gun was in my hand. And I shot." He looked at John. "And that's what happened."

John helped the shaken man to his feet and Jean ran to him. They embraced, and Chris started to cry, followed, naturally, by Jean. Over on the porch sat Ty in his chair, looking thoughtful. John wondered what he was thinking.

The other two X-men were dead. "That's five dead X-men in two days," John told his father and brother as they stood together. It began to rain a steady, soft rain. "You all better hope I kill X tomorrow morning."

"You will," Alan said without hesitation.

His father shuffled close up to John wiping rain, sweat, and dirt from his forehead. "Son, you do your best and it'll turn out alright."

John smiled weakly at his dad and nodded. Suddenly a thought jerked him hard. "Holy shit. I have no match ammo for tomorrow." He shook his head and sighed. "Man, I am just not thinking straight."

Alan and Arthur looked at one another. "Aziz," they said in unison.

"I'll take you there," Alan offered.

"No." John would have none of it. "No. You stay here. Who knows what's going to happen tonight. I'll be alright."

Assured that the perimeter was secured, and the watch re-established, John got directions to Aziz' house. He carefully squeezed into his truck and struggled to turn the key with his left hand.

The truck wouldn't start.

That did it. "You mother fucker. YOU SON OF A BITCH!" John struggled from the truck, letting loose a stream of swearing and cursing at the top of his lungs as everyone ran to see what was the matter.

"YOU ARE A GODDAM STUPID NO GOOD BASTARD TRUCK!" John reached into his holster with his good hand, pulled his .45, and emptied the whole magazine into the front fender of his truck.

"YOU GODDAM WORTHLESS PIECE OF SHIT!" he finished at last, panting heavily, glaring with hatred at the pickup truck. John turned and saw his family and friends staring open-mouthed at John, who was normally not given to outbursts. Only Jalen, who was having a laughing fit so hard that he had to lie in the grass, was not intimidated and confused by John's reaction. John stared at Jalen and, try as he might, could not suppress a smile.

He began laughing, and friends and family joined him, relieved that this odd spectacle was benign.

Ty wheeled up to him and handed him the keys to his big, and still unwashed, Dodge. "If it breaks down," he laughed, "please don't shoot it." John agreed to the terms and was soon on his way to the Arab's house.

It was only about a ten-minute drive to Aziz' place. John wondered if Aziz was his first name or last name and if he should perhaps address him as Mr. Aziz. John kept a keen eye out for mischief on the way but saw nothing, not even sentries. For a moment, he considered not stopping and driving all the way to California. He grinned at the thought. He knew there was no way out.

He came to the turnoff and followed a bumpy two-track deep into the woods. At length, he came to a large log cabin, big as a farmhouse, with a huge solar array of at least 24 big panels on a separate structure across the road. There were rusted cars and old machinery all about the property. He eased himself from the truck and knocked at the side door.

"Who's there?!" came a sudden holler from inside the hovel. "Go away."

"I'm John Wheelwright."

"I don't care if you're Zsa Zsa Gabor. It's after 11 and I sleep now."

John sighed. "I have a duel with Xavier Blount at sunrise." How strange the words sounded. "I need to load some .45. I got money."

The door creaked opened and there stood old Aziz. "You got money, eh? Don't insult me, boy. I don't need your friggin' money." He studied John for a moment and grinned, revealing bad and missing teeth. "You gonna kill X?"

"That is the plan."

"With that big ball of bandage where your hand ought to be?" the Arab laughed harshly. "You left handed?"

"No. I'm right-handed. Can I come in?"

Aziz shook his head, turned clumsily, and walked down the damp dark staircase. John followed him down through another heavy door into a spacious room that was absolutely, spotlessly clean. This was a little surprising in view of Aziz' formidable reputation as a slob.

John, even in his low and desperate state, was awed by the sight of the underground facility. "Wow," he enthused, "what a set-up."

Aziz gave him a few moments to suck in the grandeur and comprehensiveness of his reloading room, or rather, his ammunition factory.

"How come you didn't win the Gold?" Aziz broke the spell. This is why he had such an unpopular reputation.

"That English guy was better. That day." John replied, a little off guard.

"No. He wasn't."

"Not many people follow the sport."

"Your dad was real proud. Talked about it all the time. Back when the newspaper came out every day, you were in it a couple of times. Plus, I follow all that stuff, too. How's your old man?"

"He's fine. He's good... Why?"

"Well, we don't associate or nothing. But he's a gentleman," he motioned to a nearby chair. "Have a seat."

John complied, and Aziz continued.

"He never calls me 'A-rab,' or 'raghead' or any of that stuff. He always calls me Aziz. He's a gentleman. You think you gave him that heart-attack that year?"

"Jesus Christ, man," John said, annoyed. "I don't really want to talk about that with you right now."

"Suit yourself," Aziz replied. "What *do* you want?"

"I want to load a few rounds for tomorrow."

"Why a few?" Aziz asked, pulling up a chair for John and taking a seat across from him. "Don't you just get one shot?"

John stared for a few moments. "I guess so. I guess I'll just need one."

"I gotta tell you something about X. He's good. And that gun of his is a laser-beam. I *made* it a laser-beam. I also spent two months working up a load for that hand cannon of his," Aziz paused and considered John. "So, what's your strategy?"

"I don't know."

"How far away from X will you be at the duel?"

"25 yards."

"Hmm." Aziz was intent. "It's supposed to be cool tomorrow morning," he whispered to himself.

"Have you had any work done to your pistol? Whad-daya got, a Colt?"

John pulled the flat black pistol from his hip and handed it to Aziz. "It's a Series 80 with a short compensator. Trigger is beautiful, every square millimeter polished inside. Barstow barrel, Wilson springs. It's a great gun. Tight, no rattles. The gun rings. Not finicky, kind of a custom combat target gun."

Aziz was listening. He popped out the magazine and emptied the chamber with a rack of the slide. He pressed the trigger slowly until the hammer fell. "Nice." He began to strip the gun. John hopped to his feet.

"What are you doing?"

"What does it look like? Relax."

In a minute, the gun was almost completely stripped. Aziz put on a pair of glasses and began to examine the pieces meticulously. "Nice work."

John sat in silence for about ten minutes while Aziz completed his examination. Finally, he looked up.

"You've got a hairline fracture in the magazine right up here near the edge. You got a spare?"

"Yeah," John was impressed. "I got a couple."

"Yeah, well you better use one of them. Don't forget. When you get home, throw this away." Aziz held up the offending magazine. "Better yet," and Aziz tossed it into the trashcan nearby.

Aziz began to clean and reassemble the weapon. John waited patiently. Finally, a few drops of oil were applied, and the slide and barrel were put back together. Putting the loose round back in a new magazine, Aziz slammed it home, racked the slide, and snicked the safety on. He spun the gun in his hand and handed it back to John.

Then Aziz bounded out of the chair and spun to the nearest bench. Bolted to it was a modest Rock Chucker press. Aziz, looking for the moment as studious and re-fined as any college professor perusing the library stacks, scanned his cabinets full of loading dies for every caliber that John had ever seen or heard spoken of. He took down a set of RCBS dies in .45 ACP and began cleaning them with what smelled to John like acetone.

That done, he installed the first die into the green press. Aziz opened a cupboard and took out a single brass case.

"Remington?" he asked John, who nodded affirmatively.

"Primer?" Aziz queried.

"CCI."

The old Arab dropped a fresh primer into a separate little press bolted to a table nearby. He set the case atop it, pulled down the lever, pushed up, and took out the case. On his way back to the big bench he checked the seating-depth of the primer with the pad of his index finger.

"What's your recipe, son," Aziz asked John.

"5.5 grains of Bullseye and a Speer 200 grain jacketed hollowpoint. Very light crimp, bullet seated exactly to the middle of the cannelure."

Aziz had assembled the requested items in seconds. He carefully measured the powder, but not before he went to his safe and removed his check weights. They were in a wooden case lined with velvet. With these gleaming cylinders of silver metal, old Aziz checked the calibration of his scale, which, no surprise to John, needed no correction.

Aziz pulled down on the press handle until the die barely entered the neck of the brass case and carefully withdrew. Powder weighed and transferred to the case, Aziz changed dies, put a carefully examined hollowpointed bullet atop the case, and pulled the handle down again. This time, he steadied the slug atop the case until it entered the die. After another adjustment, he lowered the press again and beheld the completed round, which he removed directly and studied closely.

This process had not taken five minutes and had been executed perfectly, without a single wasted movement. Aziz turned to John.

"Here." He handed John the single cartridge. It was perfect, the crimp holding the bullet tight with an almost imperceptible caress of the case neck.

John had never in his life let anyone load his ammo. It came from a well-known ammo company or he made it himself, never otherwise. He came to Aziz's house to load some ammo himself and pay for the use of the facilities. But as he took the cartridge from the old Arab, he knew that this would suffice. If he didn't beat X tomorrow morning, it wouldn't be because of the ammunition. He stood up.

Aziz studied him. "Don't sleep tonight."

"What? I mean, I probably won't be able to if I wanted to."

"Don't want to. Stay awake." Aziz put his hands on John's shoulders and stared into his eyes with an intensity that John thought freakish.

"Sit somewhere by yourself and don't do anything. Just sit there. You are a warrior. An infidel, but a warrior. Allah will inspire your heart." Aziz released the shaken John and pushed him back in his chair. He began cleaning up the bench area.

"You're very troubled tonight; who wouldn't be. But if you do what I say, then your heart will be open to wisdom and strength. You need a plan, my young warrior, or in a few hours, you'll be dead. And so will your family and friends. And though you have chosen to take a bull by the pizzle, God is great. Sit alone all night. Don't think, just open your heart."

John listened numbly to this unexpected sermon. He needed to get out of there. He pulled himself out of the chair.

"Thanks for the cartridge, Aziz, and nice to meet you," he said weakly and started upstairs. He didn't feel himself. Once outside, he turned to wave goodnight to the strange little Arab, who called out to John.

"Take my cartridge and kill Xavier with it. You can do it. Many people would not mind to see him dead; even people who work for him."

"Goodnight, Aziz." John turned and walked to the truck.

"Allāhu akbar!" he heard Aziz bellow, as he shut the old metal door with a slam that echoed through the dark pines.

John started the truck and headed down the road toward home. He felt extremely weary and needed at least to rest if sleep would not come to him. He decided to spend the night in the library, the quietest part of the house where he could have some peace. It was all he could do to not fall asleep behind the wheel. Yes. He needed to rest.

Anger his general and confuse him.

John awoke again with a start. He had once again dozed off sitting against the wall. His arm was elevated to his side on three stacked pillows, and he was in exquisite pain.

"Oh shit," he breathed, as he got up from the bed, and began to pace about the room, clutching his bandaged hand to his chest. He dared not take anything for the agony except aspirin, which was not even putting a dent in the throbbing. He glanced over and saw "3:15" in the pale red readout of his mother's old clock, a gaudy thing with animals and ears of corn arranged in a circle about the display. This clock, which his mother had fashioned for a church bazaar (but could not sell no matter how far down she was willing to drop her asking price), was suddenly very dear to him. He thought of her.

He didn't want to sleep, he wanted to think of a way out of his extraordinary predicament, but he had exhausted himself. He had not done as Aziz had suggested, not being able to just meditate upon a solution. What if nothing would come? It wasn't like John to sit around and wait for answers. He paced back to the couch and sat again, trying not to think.

Anger his general and confuse him.

"What?" John awoke with a jolt. "Goddam it..." he moaned and then started to sob like a strong man stretched beyond his limit, who just wants the cup to pass away, begging for a Christ to come and drink it for him. He hated the religion of his parents, the religion of his youth, and wondered if there would really be any comfort for him if

155

he were a believer. He didn't think so and shook that useless thought away.

He pulled himself to the icebox and reached for a Coke, thought better of it because of the caffeine affecting his shooting, and settled for a glass of water. While he drank, he had the saddest thought of his life – he may never taste Coke again. This trite realization entered his suffering soul like a crowbar and pried him wide open. *What else would he never do again?*

He sank to the floor and wept loudly and long, facing not only death but humiliation, and fear and shame at the idea of his family at the mercy of Xavier Blount. He felt life, but no hope, and soon dozed again into the easier sleep of those who have wept.

He saw in his light doze the same pale red lights of his mother's silly clock, this time spelling out for him a simple and urgent message: *ANGER HIS GENERAL*, it said.

John opened his eyes and spoke aloud. "*And confuse him.*" He pulled himself to his feet and switched on the light. He set the lantern down on a table and searched the few shelves of Wheelwright family classics. "If it's not here I'm fucked," he whispered aloud, but even as he spoke these words he felt calm and oriented. His hand wasn't as sore, either. He found it: *The Art of War* by Sun Tsu.

That line was in here somewhere, for he remembered the book from his teenage years. He sat down on the big chair and scanned the verses and commentary. He found the passage at last.

Anger his general and confuse him. Pretend inferiority and encourage his arrogance.

If the general is obstinate and prone to anger, insult and enrage him so that he will be irritated and confused, and without a plan will recklessly advance against you.

John closed the book as a man hangs up the phone when he gets a message. He put the volume aside, closed his eyes, and rocked gently in the big chair.

12

It would be sun-up in about 20 minutes. X wheeled the big new Suburban to the edge of the clearing and parked. X and Charley, the giant and the gnome, emerged from the truck to much applause from the large crowd and walked briskly to the center of the clearing where Mike, the Referee chosen from John's team, awaited them. Mike and Skinner, X's Referee, had the previous evening measured and marked with chalk two small circles of damp earth separated by a distance of 75 feet. There the duelists would make their stand.

Never having negotiated a duel before, Alan was duped into agreeing on a sunrise duel and did not object to where the dueling stands were marked and measured. This put the rising sun into the eyes of his brother, which could be deadly in view of the impending cloudless dawn. Alan felt really stupid.

A crowd had been gathering all night, hundreds even camping out for a good look at the proceedings. X was a picture of swaggering impatience.

"That son of a bitch is late. Isn't he, Charley," X snapped at the bent old man who, with Mike, was responsible for refereeing the duel.

"That's right Xavier," Charley said, "he's late awright. But I guess we didn't say nothin' about that in the rules."

"This is a clusterfuck," X hissed and shook his head as he looked down and checked, for the tenth time, the smooth slide of his pistol.

"You only get one bullet, X," Mike teased. "That means you'll have to take your magazine out of that cannon you got there. Just one round in the chamber. That's the rules."

158

"I know the rules," X said flatly and released the magazine from the big .50 caliber. He handed it to Charley.

"We need the cartridge too, X," Mike said.

"That's right Xavier," Charley croaked. "Skinner'll load you up real formal when it's time."

Skinner, X's Second, had arrived about 4 a.m. when he realized finally that even with the help of Jack Daniels' finest, sleep would not come to him this night. He wasn't worried; he knew X could probably outdraw John even if John's hand wasn't mangled. He wondered if it was necessary to have hurt him so badly. He stood now at the little patch of earth that marked X's stand, looking it over yet again. "Come on over Skinner," Charley yelled. "You're supposed to be here for the ceremonies and loadin' an' all."

The crowd was thick. There were more than a thousand people here, mostly stay-overs from Rondayvoo, spread out on both sides of the narrow strip of ground. The aroma of campfires, morning coffee, and portapotty stink scented the pine air. Close to the action was a row of chairs on which sat the Wheelwrights and friends, the glamorous Tanya, and a few high-ranking men from X's organization. But there was no sign of John or his party.

"The sun is coming up *now*," X seethed at Mike, who stepped back guardedly. "He'll be here when he gets here, X. I don't know where the hell he is."

Only when the sun had completely cleared the shallow hill did John's mudcaked and bullet-riddled truck jerk and amble into the clearing. In the driver's seat was a fellow named Sean, a long-time family friend, with John at his side. There was a little ripple of clapping through the crowd as the pair made their way to join the other principals at the center of the field. All beheld John's right hand wrapped up like a balloon in a clean shroud of bandage.

There was something else to notice: John was wearing his gun holstered, as usual, on his right hip.

"Goddam John," Sean said, beholding the crowd. "We should have sold tickets." John laughed as the two finally joined the little group in the middle of the field.

"You're late. Where's your brother," X asked John. "Alan's supposed to be your Second. Where is he?"

John made a hawking sound and spat a thick wad of phlegm into X's face. He instantly leaped at John, who was shielded by Sean and Mike as he ran out of X's grasp, laughing and taunting him. The four riflemen, two from each team assigned to enforce the duel protocol, looked edgy and fingered the safeties of their guns. There was no provision for this, but no proscription against it. The crowd cheered loudly, enjoying the show. X, a giant by any standards, could not catch the agile John, and when he realized that the crowd was having a laugh at the slapstick comedy which he was providing, stopped chasing John and walked back to the Referees.

X was red-faced and so livid as to be speechless. John joined the group but stayed on guard for any quick movements by X.

"To answer your question," Sean spoke to X with a smirk, "Alan backed out. I don't know why, and it's none of your business anyway."

"Nothin' in the rules about if somebody backs out," Charley proclaimed importantly. "I guess if..."

"Just shut the fuck up Charley," X hissed. "Let's get on with it."

Alan was awakened by a rustle of leaves. He rubbed his eyes, sat up, and pulled his coat across his neck against the cool wind. The horizon was a pale rose, and he squinted in the half-light at the form near the base of the big birch tree about 50 yards away. Alan had guessed correctly: this was the perfect place to post a sniper. The shadowy form ambled up the old birch quickly as Alan rose from behind the fallen log, his sister's AR-15 in hand, and began his quiet stalk through the trees toward the base of the birch tree.

He reasoned that the form about 15 feet up the tree may belong to Xavier's local sharpshooter Marty, for few others could have possibly negotiated that tree with such monkey-like facility. Marty, he also knew, was an excellent shot with the fancy Weatherby, the "pimp gun," as Alan liked to call it. *Marty's too young for this shit,* Alan thought.

He maneuvered to about ten feet from the tree, hiding his form behind another large birch tree as the first colors of dawn began to spread along the horizon. The form above him was now still and settled in. The duel would soon be consummated and there was no time to dally. Alan made his move.

"Marty? Is that you?" he called up to the form above him.

"Who's that! Who's down there?" the startled voice of Marty called back.

"Now listen to me, Marty," Alan commanded. "Drop that pimp gun out of that tree right now."

"I can't. Where are you? Show yourself, goddamit. Is it you, Alan?"

"I've got a clear shot at you," Alan lied. "Marty Miller, you drop that rifle right now or I'll kill you right where you sit."

"Oh Jesus," Marty breathed as the gun started its crash through the branches, landing with an ugly thud at the base of the birch.

"Now get your worthless ass down here."

Alan tied Marty up sitting against the very tree that he had climbed. He grabbed the Weatherby by the barrel and swung it against the trunk of the birch tree. Again and again he wailed away against the tree until the pretty stock split and shattered. He laid the remains on the ground and smashed at the barrel with a large rock until it was badly bent. This was all too much for young Marty, who was crying like a child.

"You'll never use this gun against us," Alan said to him. He then noticed that Marty's pants were wet.

"You pissed your pants, Marty. How come?"

Marty sniffed and coughed. "I thought you were going to kill me up in the tree."

Alan laughed. "Shit, Marty. I don't do that sorta thing anymore."

Mission accomplished, Alan sprinted off down the trail that would take him to the dueling grounds, but before he reached the clearing heard two shots ring out and then a thousand gasping voices.

Kevin Paris looked into the rising sun, now dancing above the hilltop in full morning glory. Kevin was the west-angle sniper. He had been in position for two hours and was impatient at the delay. His spotting scope showed both duelists in position, but all the attention was on Sean, who looked like he was giving a little speech in the center of the field. He moved back to his rifle.

It was hard not to like Kevin despite his affiliation with X's gang. He was a crack shot and was distinguished as the only one around to actually have a real 'sniper rifle.' Kevin was in position on the hillside exactly 200 meters away. There was no wind, and visibility could not have been better.

The 11-pound McMillan rifle was chambered for .300 Winchester Magnum, and rested on a rockshelf, tripod extended. Kevin was comfortable and well-camouflaged. He had made this shot on melons many times when he lived at home with his folks until it became a poor economy to shoot at food. But this was the scenario he had trained for in the military and as an avocation: a sniper situation, facing a man who needed killing. He knew if John Wheelwright killed Xavier Blount that the Wheelwrights and their allies would revolt and maybe crush out X's power structure. That's what Skinner told him, anyway. Everybody hated how X lorded it over everyone, but at least there was some freedom in the area, and even the U.N. troops were afraid of X's machine.

Besides, Kevin thought, he himself had done pretty well in these times that were incredibly tough for folks. He even had a girlfriend, Connie, whom he loved and who would marry him if he asked her. He had good guns, a new truck, friends, a house of his own – hell, if it wasn't for X, there's no telling what would have become of his life. He owed all of this to X, who had never asked him for anything until now. These were the thoughts going through Kevin's mind as he waited.

He squinted again through the old and sturdy 14x Leopold scope and tried to clear his mind of the thought that he had no real personal reason to kill John Wheelwright. *But this is bigger than just me*, he reasoned. *All my friends are depending on me, and I'm not going to fail them.*

Suddenly, he hated John Wheelwright and had to wipe a distorting tear from his eye as he centered the crosshairs on John's chest exactly 620 feet away. There was something happening now. The talking had stopped. This is it. Here it is. Here it comes Oh Baby, here it comes!

That moment a shot rang out, then another.

The six men, Duelists, Seconds, and Referees, were ready to get down to business. The two pistols, empty of their magazines, were held by referees Mike and Charley. John's Second, Sean, gave Mike the single .45 ACP cartridge that John had watched Aziz load the night before. Mike inserted the cartridge into the magazine and pushed the mag into the pistol with a click. He retracted the slide and let it slam home with that familiar sound and feel that said all was well and the cartridge was now snug in its chamber. He pressed the magazine release and the now-empty magazine popped free. He pocketed the mag, snicked the safety on and gave the gun to Sean.

Likewise, Skinner handed Charley the massive .50 caliber round. Ceremoniously chambered and the pistol put on safe, Charley handed the gun to Skinner.

Mike spoke. "You each have one cartridge loaded. When you reach your stations, your Seconds will give you your pistols, and you tell them when you're ready. Then me and Charley will say when you can start the duel. Both you guys agree?" Both Duelists said they were ready, and the Seconds led their men to their stations. They each stood now in the center of their respective six-foot chalk circles 75 feet from one another, and there they must remain until the duel is over.

There was a commotion on the sideline. Grace and Andrea were punching Tanya so hard that she had fallen down, and some of X's captains had to rush to shield her. Before they could stop the assault, Tanya was deep in the mud, her face a bloody mask, and she had lost teeth in the beating. Tanya was sobbing hysterically, but X remained frozen in his chalk circle, noting John's gunmen at the corners who would have gleefully picked him off had he stepped outside the lines. John glared at X, whose eyes were bulging with indignation and frustration. This was hardly the dignified sport that X required of his negotiators, and he made a note to punish Skinner and even Charley for letting him be humiliated like this. What will Tanya think?

The sun, as feared, was right in John's eyes. Both combatants now had their pistols and each retracted the slide a bit to make sure that there really was a cartridge in place. Each duelist signaled ready. Skinner passed on X's okay to the Referees, but Sean asked to speak, a request that the Refs acknowledged.

"I believe it's sort of customary at this point to try one last time to settle this peaceably," Sean spoke in a loud, formal voice so that all could hear. The crowd wasn't too fond of this idea, like most crowds, hoping for a little bloodshed to ease life's dull routine. He continued. "If John and X would agree to consider..."

"Sean!" John barked, interrupting him in mid-sentence. "Stop." He pointed at X. "This pig needs death. Get on with it!"

The crowd cheered wildly at this new indignity – they were not to be disappointed after all. Sean shook his head and walked back toward John's chalk circle. The ready sign was given, this time by both Seconds.

There was a sudden hush, and the seconds passed slowly. Finally, X yelled to John across the distance.

"Are you going to draw or not?"

"I'm going to kill you, and while I'm at it I'm going to humiliate you, you piece of shit," John hollered back.

No one had ever talked to X like this and lived a moment longer. "Draw!" X screamed. His mind raced, but he dared not break the rules of the duel, for two of the riflemen posted at the corners would kill him where he stood.

"Listen to me, everyone!" John yelled to all present. "X's thugs attacked my family's home and killed our livestock. They ruined my hand two nights ago." The crowd fell silent in rapt attention. "To punish him, and to humiliate him on his way to hell, I'm going to draw from my right hip with my left hand and shoot him dead before he can clear his holster. I'm going to do this with the sun in my eyes," John paused dramatically. "And I'm going to give him the draw."

"All bets are off!" was the cry throughout the crowd, and only the rapidly unfolding drama prevented the crowd from rioting to recover their money.

Xavier was clearly angry and off guard. "That's not possible for you to do that," he said through clenched teeth.

"Talking dead man." John shouted back. "Draw."

Ferocious X went to his gun faster than he had ever done before. He pulled harder than he ever had, brought the big pistol to bear with spectacular swiftness, and made it roar.

At X's first movement, John methodically reached his left hand around to the Colt on his other hip and carefully coaxed the pistol out, stooping a bit. John didn't hear the Desert Eagle's big blast. He slowly brought his pistol to a careful aim, pressed the trigger, and saw X stiffen and slam backward with a plop onto the wet earth.

From his well-hidden perch, Kevin saw his boss on the ground through the riflescope and quickly trained the crosshairs back onto the chest of John Wheelwright. He snicked the safety off. In a flash, he knew that Connie would never marry him; that he would have to give up his house now and pack up all he could carry in his new truck, leaving behind his old life, and hit the road. He could not kill John Wheelwright because he admired him, but he could not stay in Deer Park because he had betrayed his friends. He put his head into his hands and wept bitterly.

Tanya ran from the sidelines and threw herself on Xavier Blount's body. She lifted her still bleeding face to the sky and wailed, *"I killed him! I killed him!"* John stood in the chalk circle and swayed back and forth, only now becoming aware of the hot sting in his shoulder. She was right, he thought. She *did* kill him. Rather, she let John kill him. He sank to his knees, as in slow-motion, hardly aware of the people that now surrounded him, helping him to his feet and embracing him. The roar in his head was the crowd, showing their appreciation for a good show.

John saw Alan's face among those who pressed upon him. "Where were you?" John said weakly to his brother, who was panting from the long sprint.

"I was busy."

"Is X dead?"

"Through the mustache; no exit hole," Mike smiled at John.

John gave a great gasp of relief, turned and saw the sweet face of Grace trying to get to him, and passed out.

When he came to, he was in the truck, sitting between Grace and Alan, and noticed that he had already been bandaged. "No hospital," he groaned.

"You don't need to," Alan said cheerfully. The bullet had cut a deep groove across John's left shoulder blade, right down to the bone. "Remember the surgeon that you had at Escanaba?"

John nodded.

"Well, he was there at the duel," Alan said. "He looked at the wound and said he'd meet us at the farm to take care of it."

"Why do I feel so groggy."

"Drugs," Alan replied. "That doctor came prepared, man, I'll tell you what. He figured if you lived through this, you were going to need him."

"Well," John smiled wanly. "At least the left side of my body is as painful as the right side now."

He stayed awake the last half hour of the drive, and when they arrived at the farm, they saw that the celebration had already begun. It was open house at the Wheelwrights. X was dead, and Arthur had just paid off the farm, which he hoped was now free from the threat of assault by X's organization. No one felt like examining that premise too very closely this day.

The doctor was a cheerful, baby-faced young man with a lot of experience in wound repair as a surgeon in the Mid-East wars. While cleaning, stitching, and bandaging John's shoulder, he regaled him with stories from Mexico, where he was stationed during a bloody peasant uprising that the blue helmets were obliged to put down. That was his first job after his orthopedic residency was completed. By the time the last tale was told, and the bandage was secure, John's wound seemed pretty trivial after all. His arm was immobilized to the elbow by the big bandage.

When he descended the stairs on the arm of Grace to greet his family and friends, he was hailed as if he were a prince come to court after a great victory. People whom he had never seen before were there to pay their respects, some of whom Alan knew to be former X-men. Alan kept an eye on these fellows and had each subjected to a frisk. They were all clean, and a little offended, Alan noted with some amusement.

At the foot of the stairs, his father embraced him, and John realized how happy he was to do something for Arthur and to have done it right.

"Arthur, where did all this beer come from?" John motioned with his bandaged hand to the three kegs on the screened porch.

"Goddam Ty," Arthur laughed. "He has a ton of this stuff squirreled away.

"I knew you'd win, and, well, we had to have beer," Ty said. "This is a good occasion. Christ, look around!"

There must have been 200 people there, and John would spend the next hour receiving the homage of the crowd. Grace sat with him, beaming proudly.

Ty and Arthur sat together now, laughing and bantering about the old times. All animosity between them had been banished by the events of the last week, and John's heart was gladdened by this. Andrea joined the dancing in the dining room with a young man no one had seen before, but no one doubted that she would be treated on the dance floor with the greatest deference. Jalen, John noted with some distress, had learned to play chess for money, and had still yet to lose a game since his arrival at the farm. When he saw John, he dug into his pocket and with a toothy grin brandished a wad of bills for John to admire. John tried hard to make a stern face and shook his head. He reminded himself to have a talk with Jalen about that.

The crowd peaked about 8 pm, and by midnight, only the family and a few good friends remained. The house was a mess, but Arthur had never seen such a beautiful sight as his farm that night. It was a happy place, and it was his, by God. *And by John,* he smiled, puffed with fatherly love and pride.

Jean and Chris were rather conspicuous by their absence for most of the evening, and when they reappeared, it was through the back door from the garden. Ty wheeled himself into the small sitting room off the living room area and called Chris in to see him. Jean looked nervously at her poet and drew herself a beer from the one good keg. As Chris entered the sitting room, Ty tripped him with his cane, and Chris landed flat on his ass against the wall, then onto the floor. Ty wheeled to him in a flash, grabbed him by the topknot of his grey head with his left fist, and in his right hand gleamed his Randall Model 1. He held the blade to the poet's throat. The others, except for Arthur, who stepped out, ran to the doorway agog at the sight.

"So, you think that I'm not just crippled, but I'm blind, too, eh?" Chris felt the razor-sharp edge of the big knife dance and scrape on his Adam's apple.

"I don't even think you're crippled!" the poet squeaked.

"Have you been making love to my woman?" Ty bellowed as he pulled up on Chris's hair as if to expose more of his ruddy pink neck. "I SAID HAVE YOU BEEN MAKING LOVE TO MY JEAN!?" he roared.

Jean stepped forward. "Oh, please, Ty, don't."

"STAY BACK!" Ty turned his head and barked at Jean, spitting saliva in his rage. She fell back onto Andrea, biting her knuckles and quaking in fear.

Chris swallowed hard and felt the blade slide over his throat. "Yes." He gulped again and closed his eyes tightly. "I love Jean. And if you kill me, I'll still love her, and she'll still love me."

At that, Ty spun the knife edge-out and pressed the dull side into Chris' neck. The poet gurgled a scream and froze. Ty pulled the knife back and grinned a big grin. "If you gave me any other answer, I'd have sawed your head clean off." He wheeled back, helped the poet to his feet and extended his hand to Chris. "No hard feelings?"

"No," Chris patted his hair down and sighed. "No hard feelings." He managed a weak smile. Jean came to Ty and kissed him full on the lips. She turned, and Ty swatted her rear hard as she left the room. She smiled at him over her shoulder as she rejoined Andrea and Grace. Chris bolted upstairs. Alan turned to John.

"You know, that's the second guy I saw piss his pants today." The brothers laughed, and Alan helped John struggle to his feet. Alan whispered to John, "You really weren't dumb enough to risk a head-shot on X from 25-yards, were you?"

John grimaced. Alan was not fooled. "Actually, I was aiming for his chest. Guess the shot went a little high," he said sheepishly.

"*A little high!*" Alan chuckled and patted his big brother on the shoulder. "It'll be our little secret. And it would never occur to me to blackmail you with this little factoid for the rest of your life."

John laughed. "I know I can count on you."

Arthur popped his head around the hallway corner and interrupted the boys with an urgent whisper. "Come down to the basement," he said. "There are a couple of people you need to see. I put them down in the laundry room and told them to wait for you." With that cryptic comment, Arthur eyed his sons with a foreboding aspect.

Alan led the way and John followed down to the basement and into the laundry room, where they beheld a cleaned-up, if badly bruised and partly toothless, Tanya. Behind her stood X's number two man, Skinner himself.

Alan spoke first. "Well! This is a surprise. Remember me telling you that you either had balls like cantaloupes or else you're one dumb son of a bitch?"

"I recall I admitted to a little of both," Skinner smiled. He reached out a laudatory hand to John. "Congratulations on your victory in the duel."

John refused the handshake. "What do you want, Skinner? What are you doing here?"

Skinner dropped his arm then put his hands on Tanya's shoulders. "We have a proposition," he said.

John looked hard. "You are in no position to proposition me."

"Just hear me out."

John nodded. "Go ahead."

"You killed the King," Skinner said, and let that sink in for a moment.

"You plan on taking the spoils?" John asked.

"I don't want the spoils. I think you should have them. I already explained: I'm not a killer. Or a King. I just-"

Alan interrupted. "You just don't want to lose what you had, right? If X was King, you were the Crown Prince."

"I don't want the crown," Skinner said. "I want John to have it, and I could make the transition very smooth. You could move in tomorrow."

John shook his head. "I'm not-"

"Let me finish." Skinner paused. "X, for all his savageries and flaws, created a nation within a nation. It *needs* a King. And if it isn't you, then there will be war. I can think of a dozen well-placed hotheads, with twice X's cruelty and none of his intelligence, that would do anything – and I mean *anything* – to take over what X built. But the devastation would be so immense that no one would be untouched by it. But you! You could walk in and take the helm unchallenged. Don't you see?"

"With you as my Number Two man."

"It would be the smart move," Skinner said. "I know everything about this organization. And to have it be run

172

by a man like you, a good man out for the good of others – there would be no stopping us."

John nodded, seeming to consider this royal offer. He looked at Tanya, all this while standing perfectly still and gazing at John with hope and wonder in her countenance.

"What about you?" he asked. "What are you doing here?"

"To beg for your mercy." Clear and bright with that Russian tang.

John chuckled. "Really? And why should I offer you this?"

"Because you are a good man. Because if I hadn't caused the duel to happen, you and your family would probably be dead."

Alan whistled in wonder. "Wow! I thought Skinner was the one with the balls."

Tanya went on. "Skinner told me I should come with him because you could be a better King than X and you might pardon me to show what a merciful man you are."

Skinner coughed and gave Tanya a scornful look. "Or something like that."

"Much to consider," John said. "I'll give your proposal the consideration it merits."

"Thanks for hearing us," Skinner said.

"So!" Alan said. "We done here?"

John grinned at his little brother. "I believe we are."

"Good." Alan pulled from his coat a Ruger .22 with an attached suppressor, fired two quiet rounds into Skinner's forehead, and before Tanya could work up a scream, Alan attempted to serve her likewise. As he pulled the trigger, John swept Alan's arm up and away, and the bullet landed in the ceiling.

"What the *hell?*" Alan was indignant.

"No," John said flatly. "Not her." Alan stood down as John turned her attention to the quaking woman.

"Get out," he said. "Now. I spare your life. Get out of this house and don't ever let me see you again."

At this reprieve, Tanta turned and sprinted out the door and down the hallway, yelling "Thank you! Thank you!" all the way to the staircase.

Alan considered his brother. "Really?" he asked.

"She's just a silly whore," John explained. "Plus, she's right. If it weren't for her, we'd all be dead."

"Yes," Alan said sarcastically, "Her benevolence was overwhelming."

John laughed. "Look at you and your big words!"

"Oh, shut up," Alan laughed. He poked at the body of the dead Skinner with his foot. "Sorry, King John, but this guy needed killing."

"Agreed," John said. "He was evil."

They stood for a moment in the deathly silence. "Guy did have balls, though," John said. He looked at Alan. "You just happened to have a suppressed 22 in your coat?"

Alan held the gun up for display. "I thought there might be trouble tonight, and if there was, I didn't want to make a lot of noise."

"Nice suppressor," John said. "That new?"

"Got it at the Rondayvoo."

"Uh huh," John said. "So you just happened to have the perfect weapon on you? What a guy."

"Totally serendipitous," Alan replied and stood uncomfortably. He looked at his brother. "Is that a word?"

John hunted his lover upstairs. He felt a need. She was chatting with Chris, who had since changed his pants and rejoined the festivities. John sought Grace's arm and together they walked outside, hearing Ty and Arthur laughing lusty and long as the happy couple strolled through the garden and into the darkness of the fields.

At length, they halted. John turned to Grace. "I can't hug you," he said.

"You'll hug me again soon," she whispered and leaned against his chest. He stroked her hair and kissed the top of her head, breathing in her scent with the cool pine air.

"Will you marry me?" Grace asked John. He laughed and took a step back.

"You are incredible," he said. "I'm supposed to ask *you* that."

"I know, but I couldn't wait."

"Is that right? What makes you think I was going to ask you?"

She leaned her head against his chest again and laughed. "O you! Don't make bad jokes like that."

"I don't have any money, you know," John said. "I want to do it right and, well, *normal* for once. I want to get you a nice diamond ring, for instance."

"I don't want to be normal," Grace looked into his eyes. "And you do it right, John." She looked up into the sky. "You just love me, and these will be our diamonds."

John looked up into the black sky and together they gazed with wonder, bound together in their love and bathed in the dazzling diamond-dust of a trillion stars.

ᘓᘔ

About Gerald Brennan

I was born on September 2, 1953, in Jessup, PA. At age two I moved to Dearborn, MI, where I lived with my family until my late teens. The eldest of six children, I went to Catholic school, and when my brain started working at about age 15, I left the Church, my youthful mind appalled by its many dogmas. Nor did the priests and nuns wish to indulge my curious nature. When we had philosophical questions, the answer was usually along the lines of "Shut up." It was in high school that I began to write down the music in my head.

Wandering in the desert for many years, I drank heavily, experimented with drugs, and studied music, science and philosophy. Though I never had any formal music education, living in Ann Arbor put many wonderful resources at my disposal, including many fine Steinway grands sprinkled merrily throughout the University of Michigan campus back in the day when there didn't need to be a lock on every door.

I became a good pianist in the following years, as well as composer. I had many musical adventures—breaking a Steinway grand playing Liszt at the University of Michigan music school, playing Liszt's American Steinway at the Smithsonian Museum in an impromptu recital that drew quite a wondrous crowd.

I became a National Public Radio affiliate producer with WUOM, WVGR and WFUM out of the U-M. I produced hundreds of weekly programs in my decade there—including *The Musical Theatre, New Music, New Releases, From the Monophonic Era, Music of Our World, Excursions* and *Nocturne.*

In 1980 I organized the Ann Arbor-based Sinewave Studios for the development and propagation of new art music. I produced about 20 concerts and conducted the North American premiere of Karlheinz Stockhausen's *Für kommende zeiten* at the Detroit Institute of Art.

My writing career started in 1984 when I wrote and self-published a booklet on starting a classical record collection. Borders Books agreed to carry it, and it finally made its way into the paws of a publisher. They asked me to expand it into a sure enough book and thus was born *Classical Records, Starting Your Collection.* After it was published, I took it to the Ann Arbor News and asked them if they needed a music reviewer. Turned out they did, and so, all while I had the radio gig, I was reviewing the best acts in the world that came through town.

Before all that I worked in record stores, including the famous Liberty Music. I also sold pianos, moved pianos, sold sheet music, managed U-M's record and sheet music store, and wrote for various national music journals.

In 1998, I was headhunted by a visionary fellow named Michael Erlewine, who decided that it would be a good idea to get hold of every album in the world and put every bit of information about it into a database. Eventually the idea included taking a photo of the album and doing sound samples. They started with a core of a few music geeks and began by going through their own collections. The company Erlewine founded was called *All Media Guide* (www.allmusic.com), which became the world's largest repository of product data and editorial information about music.

Erlewine asked me to assume the post of Director of Content of Classical Music at AMG, to create a department that would be devoted to classical music. I jumped at it, and in four years my amazing staff and I, along with scores of excellent writers, amassed the data, created the classical website, and produced the giant reference book, *AMG Guide to Classical Music,* which I edited and saw published in 2005. My mission was accomplished; my staff was a well-oiled machine and easily the best and happiest of all AMG's departments. Then 'investor fatigue' set in among the shareholders and AMG was appointed a slick new president who knew little about what we did or why but was hired to sell the company at a good price to whomever, and fast. He instinctively disliked me and my open resistance to his schemes and I was fired. I had no hard feelings. I had completed my mission, and it was time to go.

Now I write music and books, make recordings, and give the rare recital.

Books include this one, also *The Complete Short Stories;* the recent *The Angel Jophiel*, a fantasy novel about the classical music world and an angel sent to Earth to help rejuvenate the dying Arts, and *A Song of Blood and Ashes,* a vampire tale set in contemporary Ireland and Ann Arbor. Also, *Classical Music & Recordings—a primer,* and *Views & Reviews - Chronicles from the Twilight of the Golden Age of Classical Music.* I have also written a memoir of sorts, called *There was this guy once...*

Musically, I've to date got 90 songs published in three *SongBooks*, several chamber and orchestral pieces, piano works, a full-length Broadway-style musical called *Penelope*, choral works, *Anticanon* for orchestra, and a large orchestral piece called *Sinfonia Matrix,* which requires some 80-octillion years to be heard in its entirety. Therefore, performance versions are extracted depending upon available forces, duration required, and occasion.

Available recordings include *Mythos* (piano pieces based upon Greek myth characters, recorded in recital and in-studio), *Five Fantasy Nocturnes for piano, Campfire—The Burning Psaltery* (a phantasmagorical piece for an innocent 12-string psaltery), *7 Solo Songs from 'Penelope,'* and more than 60 songs *From the SongBooks* recorded in studio and at home, by me and various performers.

Also available on CD is the electronically-based Ambient Music Series, which includes *Ambient Counterpoint, Grand Starbells, Monochrome Frescos, The Singing Moon,* and *Whisperings of Angels.*

All items detailed above are published by DreamStreet Press and available on Amazon or through DreamStreetPress.com.

OTHER BOOKS BY GERALD BRENNAN

JOPHIEL

Jophiel, Angel of the Beauty of the Divine Presence, incarnates in a mid-western town to a lovely woman and her outlaw husband in this tale set in near-future America.

PRINCE OF PINES

Pure unapologetic dystopian male-adventure, intelligent and well-crafted, with plenty of guns and interesting women.

THE COMPLETE SHORT STORIES

Contemporary tales in many different genres.

SONG OF BLOOD & ASHES

An ancient Vampire finally creates a protégé after centuries of searching. Blinded by her beauty and innocence, his choice was unwise. She loves a 'mortal' who does not reciprocate her affection. Her depraved appetites provoke a most horrifying catastrophe.

CLASSICAL MUSIC & RECORDINGS

This book is intended as an introduction to the species of art music which we call Classical Music.

VIEWS & REVIEWS

This book contains the original unedited versions of Gerald Brennan's previews, reviews, and interviews of the finest classical music soloists, ensembles, and orchestras in the world during what may well be looked back upon as the final flowering of Classical Music in the West.

THERE WAS THIS GUY ONCE...

There is no plot but many characters. Not exactly autobiography, but a case could be made. This is a book about the people, influences, hopes, fears, and favorite things about my life as a composer, novelist, journalist, performing musician, and person.